He was a stranger who walked through his world in a far different way from how she walked through hers.

A man who broke rules and hearts and jaws and barely looked back as he did so. He lived in a way her mother had and in a way that she herself would never choose to, not in a thousand years.

Esther sought safety and shelter in the quiet corners of society, a place that protected those who did not stray. She was a woman of common sense and good judgment, traits that she clung to tenaciously because her childhood had contained so little of either.

No, the beautiful Oliver Moreland was not the man for her. She needed to be careful around him, because under his dark blue glance, things moved inside her breast and lower that had no business being there. She swore she would choose a man wisely and any dreams of someone else needed to be squashed down with fervor.

SOPHIA JAMES

The Debutante's
Secret

HARLEQUIN
HISTORICAL

Recycling programs
for this product may
not exist in your area.

ISBN-13: 978-1-335-72323-9

The Debutante's Secret

Copyright © 2022 by Sophia James

For questions and comments about the quality of this book,
please contact us at CustomerService@Harlequin.com.

Harlequin Enterprises ULC
22 Adelaide St. West, 41st Floor
Toronto, Ontario M5H 4E3, Canada
www.Harlequin.com

Printed in U.S.A.

Sophia James lives in Chelsea Bay, on the North Shore of Auckland, New Zealand, with her husband, who is an artist. She has a degree in English and history from Auckland University and believes her love of writing was formed by reading Georgette Heyer on vacations at her grandmother's house. Sophia enjoys getting feedback at Facebook.com/sophiajamesauthor.

Books by Sophia James

Harlequin Historical

Christmas Cinderellas
"Christmas with the Earl"
The Spinster's Scandalous Affair
The Debutante's Secret

The Penniless Lords

Marriage Made in Money
Marriage Made in Shame
Marriage Made in Rebellion
Marriage Made in Hope
Once Upon a Regency Christmas
"Marriage Made at Christmas"

The Society of Wicked Gentlemen

A Secret Consequence for the Viscount

Gentlemen of Honor

A Night of Secret Surrender
A Proposition for the Comte
The Cinderella Countess

Secrets of a Victorian Household

Miss Lottie's Christmas Protector

Visit the Author Profile page
at Harlequin.com for more titles.

For Sofia, Emmerson and Isobel.

My strong little female warriors
with all the world before them.

May you find resilience and courage in
your lives and delight in your choices.

Prologue

London—December 1809

He found them on the street in the darkness, a woman and a child, huddled up in a portico against the frame of a door, snow around their feet.

They did not look like the usual homeless. They were too clean for one and too well dressed for another.

'Can I take you anywhere?' he said as the woman started to cry, the little girl behind her standing and tipping her head up to his.

'Mama and I need to go to Camden Town, sir.' She said this in a voice that held no trace of the streets whatsoever.

Camden Town was a good hour away and it was already eleven thirty at night, but the desperation he saw on the youngster's face had its own brand of urgency and he found that he could not disappoint her.

'My carriage is just here.'

'You will take us, sir?' Surprise marked her words.

'I will.'

He saw how the girl helped her mother, saw the pain in the older woman's face as she ascended the steps and sat down.

'Are you hurt, ma'am?'

'I am…fine.'

For the first time the woman spoke. There was blood on her bottom lip where it had split and bruises around one eye.

'I could find you a doctor—' he said, but the child stopped him.

'Mama just wants to be home, sir. It will be safer there.'

'Very well.'

He handed them each a blanket from the small chest to one side of the conveyance, rebuckling the leather straps as he finished. The child snuggled into hers, but the woman left the other untouched beside her on the seat.

She was a beautiful woman but weary, the lines on her face showing him that her life had been a hard one and that she had no mind at all for small talk. He wondered if he should offer her brandy from his flask, but decided against it. She looked like a female who might have been on the hard end of drunkenness and he did not wish to frighten her further.

His evening in the wilder clubs of London suddenly seemed shallow, a small world of excessive privilege bounded by one of much greater need. He also felt anxious to be rid of them, to have them gone away from his notice, gone to become someone else's problem and not his.

His own mother would have undoubtedly been disappointed by such thoughts, but she had been dead for years now, her eternal melancholy finally assuaged by a simple walk into a very deep pond.

Shaking his head, he stopped thinking just as the child spoke.

'Mama wants to know if we can pay you, sir?'

'Pay me?' Now this was unexpected.

The girl brought a ring from her pocket, a small thin gold band, and held it out to him.

'No. I don't require payment.'

She looked back at her mother and he saw the woman frown.

Unsure now as to what she should do, the child merely lowered her hand and left the bauble there in the middle of her gloveless palm. An offering she could neither give away nor take back.

The mother continued to look down, her eyes hooded, as if she might simply shake off the world by not seeing it. No one spoke after that.

Forty minutes later they reached Camden Town.

'Just here.' The girl indicated their destination as she scanned a row of buildings and he banged on the carriage roof.

When the conveyance stopped and the door was opened from outside, the pair simply stood and descended, the weather worse here than it had been in the city, the snow falling in large clumps and the temperature dropping. The girl turned to thank him, gratitude evident in her clear green eyes.

Then they were gone, swallowed up by the night,

the blankets left on the seat they had departed, a smell of lavender in the air. He did not know who they were and they had no idea as to who he was. When his footman asked whether they should now return to the city, he nodded and leant back in the seat as he felt the horses gain speed.

He hoped they would find safety. He hoped someone would help them. He hoped that right now they were being welcomed into a house offering warm food and a comfortable bed.

When he lifted the unfolded blanket from the seat the ring tumbled to the floor in front of him, the token left despite his refusal. Picking it up, he noticed initials and a date engraved inside.

M.P. 1796

As he pocketed the bauble, he stared out of the window. It had been years since he had briefly left the small enclave in London's city centre, his father's death necessitating a return home to Hampshire.

He had stayed long enough after the funeral to keep up appearances, but there was nothing left there for him any more, nothing to hold on to and become a part of.

He'd been wild and dissolute for a long while, he supposed, and in truth this sort of degeneracy needed to change into something less self-destructive. He also needed to make money to pay back his creditors and he wanted to find a peace that had been missing from his life, his riotous parties providing much of the fodder for gossip in society.

Tonight had been some sort of pointer towards the harsher realities of others, and the child's expression had been full of a feeling he had often seen in his own.

Fear and disappointment. The combination was exhausting.

He wished he could have turned his carriage around just to make certain that the pair had found shelter, but of course he could not. They would no doubt be horrified to find him following them and they had already made it plain that they needed nothing more.

Glancing at his watch, he saw it to be quarter to one. Still early. Normally he would have asked to be dropped off at one of his clubs, but tonight he had no heart for it.

God. The eyes of the child had got to him somehow, made him re-evaluate his own journey, made him think that perhaps one day he might end up homeless and drunk and in some far-off godforsaken place, reliant on the goodwill of strangers, if he kept travelling on the path he followed.

Sorrow and guilt surfaced, too.

He had not lived his life well.

The snow returned as they got nearer to the city and he swallowed away an old grief that had never left him.

Chapter One

1815

Miss Esther Barrington-Hall was swept into the light and the dancing and the movement, people all around her, the first true outing of her Season everything that her aunt had promised it would be.

She had never seen so many people gathered in one place and the sound from a quartet of talented musicians perched on a small stage nearby filled the room—'Calder Fair', a familiar tune her aunt enjoyed and had learnt to play on the piano at Redworth Manor over the last few months.

Esther's dress was one of white silk and embroidered in a darker shade, the patterns of leaves and flowers repeated all over the garment. It was by far her favourite gown of the many her aunt had procured for her, a floaty fantasy dress which invoked wood sprites or fairies, all the stories she had loved to read as a young child wrapped up in the beautiful fabric.

As she walked she felt people's notice, but her aunt bade her to simply look ahead.

'They will come to you, my dear, when the timing is right, but for now we shall make them wonder. Don't smile too much and don't speak to anyone unless they are properly introduced to you. Don't walk too fast, either. It is better to do everything slowly and correctly so that we may recognise whom we wish to.'

Don't. Don't. Don't.

How many of these warnings had she heard across the last years in the preparation for this night? One chance to get it right, to make a favourable first impression, and this was it.

The Marriage Market.

Even the name was terrifying, but if you failed at the game you were left on a shelf somewhere, high and dry for life. Or even worse, you became stuck with a husband whom you loathed.

Aunt Mary looked as regal as usual, but Esther could feel her nervousness. Not as detached as she might make out, then, and she was glad her five cousins were all here beside her, to help her out, to lean on, to smile with, to find reassurance.

Aiden would ask her to dance if no one else did and so would Jeremy, though with a little less enthusiasm, she suspected, given he had never taken to the art. Sarah and Charlotte would stay close, too. She caught Charlotte's eye at the thought and her cousin smiled at her, her warm brown eyes encouraging.

Family.

For so very long she had had none and now she

was full to overflowing. Benjamin, the oldest, would be here somewhere as well, and on his best behaviour under the strict orders of his mother.

'A united front is what is needed,' Aunt Mary had impressed on them all before they had left their town house in St James's. 'There will be no shirking away, Ben. Do you understand me? We need every one of you at your posts to make sure that this evening will be the success for Esther that I envisage it to be and we cannot afford errors.'

Cannot afford gossip.

Because under the calm lay a chasm, a rip in the passing of time, a rent that could turn all plans awry if they were not careful.

Every member of the Barrington-Hall family understood that, implicitly, and they were all doing their very best to see that Esther stayed safe.

Uncle Thomas had joined them now, too, his bearing adding to the blend. He was a tall and confident man, his title, wealth and connections allowing him the sort of ease in society that others found beguiling.

'You will do fine here, Esther, and on your own account. Just be yourself. You are a girl of good sense and reason.'

The words made her smile because before he had found her in the orphanage in London town and brought her back to Kent, she had had no idea at all as to who that was—the child of a mother who had veered so violently off the pathways of propriety and into the underbelly of a dangerous city.

Her aunt did not need to tell her how easily a

woman could be ruined by not taking notice of the many and unwritten rules of society. No, they were etched in blood upon her very soul and if ever there was a girl who had little tolerance for poor behaviour and breaking the rules it was indeed her.

Her aunt had stopped before a woman of remarkable beauty despite her age, with a young man beside her who held the same sort of elegant bone structure in his face.

'Lady Beaumont.'

'Lady Duggan.'

There was a momentary sizing up of costume, hairstyle and intention before the other spoke.

'It is good to see you here. I thought perhaps you were still in the country at Redworth?'

'No, we are here in town for the Season of our youngest niece. Lady Beaumont, may I introduce Miss Esther Barrington-Hall to you?'

Dipping into the expected curtsy, Esther smiled. Not too sunnily and not with too much confidence. Just the right amount of modesty without appearing simpering. Was that not what Aunt Mary had instructed her to do time after time?

The other woman looked pleased.

'A pleasure to meet you, my dear, and this is my son, Lord Alberton. He is newly arrived back from a journey to the Americas and we are very glad indeed to have him home.'

'Miss Barrington-Hall.' Lord Alberton took her hand and held it for a moment. 'I am delighted to meet you.'

His charm was effortless, the smile accompanying his words both genuine and kind.

'I wonder if I might petition you for the next dance before you are swamped with offers and there are none left over.'

He'd moved back a little now, allowing her some space. He was careful in his words and his actions and she liked this. A man who knew the rules and would stick by them. A man who would not transgress from what was proper and right.

'Indeed, my lord.' She found her dance card and pen and wrote his name on the first line. A waltz. She hoped her aunt would allow it, but it seemed she was more than pleased as she simply stood by and observed their exchange.

Her first dance out in society and to a young lord who was handsome and tall. The evening could not look finer.

'Benjamin, your cousin, is a friend of mine and he specifically asked me to watch out for you this evening, Miss Barrington-Hall. I admit after meeting you that I am more than willing to do so, for the task is not an onerous one at all.'

'Thank you. It is rather daunting to be in the company of so many people. Of course we have gatherings in the country in Kent, but they are small compared to this one.'

'Use them as a practice,' he returned, 'My sister was more than overcome when she first came into society, but is now married to the Earl of Thornton and very happily so.'

Esther nodded. 'How is it you know my cousin Ben?'

'We were at Eton together and then went up to the same university.'

'Cambridge?'

He nodded. 'I enjoy learning.'

She did, too, though she was not sure under the circumstances that she should tell him such, for women were not expected to revel in academia.

She was about to ask him another question when a ripple of conversation emanating through the room surprised her and she looked around. A tall man in black was walking down the stairs and everyone was peering in his direction. From this distance she could not quite make out his features, but there was something about him that was daunting yet thrilling at the very same time and she could understand the reaction of all those around her.

'That's Mr Oliver Moreland,' her companion said. 'Back to find yet another consort for his evening's pleasure,' he added, his face full of censure. 'If there is anyone whom your cousin might say to be wary of it is him, for he breaks every rule in society with impunity and somehow gets away with it. His wealth and parentage, second son to an earl, helps, I suppose, but…' He tailed off.

'But…?' Esther prompted.

'He comes from a family who have had their various detractors. It is said his mother drowned herself to find an escape from them all, his father, the Earl, following her a few years after in an alcoholic haze.'

Her face must have shown him she was shocked and so he quickly tried to mop up the damage.

'But I have said too much and I really should not have. Moreland, in truth, is a mystery and it is better to leave him well alone.' As the opening strains of the first dance filled the air he bowed to her. 'This is my dance, I believe, Miss Barrington-Hall.'

When he put out his hand she took it, enjoying the closeness of his grasp as he led her to the floor.

A waltz. A dance that allowed both partners things that no other did. A dance that she had only ever practised with her boy cousins in the blue salon at home in Kent.

She saw the man Lord Alberton had told her about far to the edge of the room, his height allowing her to keep a track of his movements. She wondered why she would be interested in glancing his way given his terrible reputation, but there was something about him that was familiar and she could not put her finger quite upon it. The puzzle intrigued her.

'Who is she? The girl in white?' Oliver Moreland asked this question of his good friend Frederick Bronson, who stood with him on the edge of the dance floor.

'Miss Esther Barrington-Hall. She is the niece of Lord and Lady Duggan and is newly arrived into London society.'

The girl was beautiful, there was no doubt of that, with her honey-blonde hair and willowy figure, but there was something in her bearing that was undeniably sensual, too. She was an excellent dancer for one, but the way she tilted her head…

Did he know her from somewhere?

'This is her first London ball, I am told.' Frederick's voice came from a distance. 'She is a stickler for propriety and is here to net herself a husband. I have heard Miss Barrington-Hall follows rules by the letter and is never happier than when in the company of her numerous cousins.'

Oliver laughed. 'Then I should find Hetty Palmer instead and see how long it takes for her to suggest something outrageous.'

'As outrageous as going home with you and jumping into a warm bed.'

'Or repairing to my carriage, which is standing just outside. Her husband has never minded.'

'Because he is a man of loose morals.'

'You say that as if it is a bad thing?'

'I say it to incite caution, Oliver. One day you will be caught by a jealous spouse and facing the possibility of a duel at dawn.'

'Oh, hardly,' he drawled, 'for if there is one thing I have always been, it is careful. Besides, I am an excellent shot.'

Frederick chuckled. 'Then instead I should wish you to be completely thrown into the arms of the god Eros and have your heart twisted in the same way you manage so easily to do with the many women of your acquaintance.'

Oliver frowned at the words. Frederick was one of his oldest friends, and such a damning hope stung.

'I have never hurt anyone, Freddie, and I am always generous when I leave. Besides, the women I enjoy are hardly new to the art of love. I would not, for instance, meddle with a virgin.'

'Then why are you still observing Miss Barrington-Hall so closely?'

Oliver dragged his eyes away.

'The flush of innocence has its own allure, I suppose. To look, but not to touch. She is surrounded by cousins, I see, and Lord and Lady Duggan are people who presumably know their duty by her.'

'Indeed, Duggan is a lord of singular reputation and one with a great propensity for protecting his family. I believe he would string you up on the nearest gallows were you to encroach upon his unblemished and cherished niece.'

Oliver nodded and took a glass from the tray being carried around by a servant dressed in a colour he could barely describe. A sort of green-yellow. Like a particularly radiant lime. On looking about he saw many other unusually shaded fabrics draping the room.

'Do our hosts have a penchant for fabric no one else would buy?'

Frederick frowned. 'I forget you were not here last year...' He tailed off.

Oliver had not been anywhere much last year because his brother, Phillip, had finally given up on reprimands and censure and pulled out a gun and shot him instead. In the side, at least, though Oliver was certain he'd been aiming for his heart.

He'd told no one what had happened, but he knew Frederick had had an inkling of him being in danger because he'd arrived without announcement at their family home, Elmsworth Manor, in Hampshire. His friend had summoned a doctor and then taken him back to the city, away from the family estate, far from the hatred. Freddie had wanted him to involve the law in the scandal, but the Moreland name still held some respectability and Oliver did not wish to ruin the last remaining remnants of it. He'd not seen his brother since.

Josephine Campbell joined them now, her fingers placed across his arm exuding pressure and allowing a silent message to be transmitted between them.

He'd slept with her a few months earlier and did not wish to resurrect the relationship. For one, her children were more than strange and, for two, she had the sort of look in her eyes that implied desperation.

So instead he asked her to dance—one dance and he would have done his duty. No one would expect him to offer more. Josephine's petite frame had once attracted him, but now the effort of bending to listen to what she had to say was less appealing. His side still ached when it rained and tonight the weather was filthy. He wondered just what he was doing here at a ball that was so obviously full of debutantes as he came through the crowd to the dance floor, Josephine holding on to him in a way that intimated she might never let go.

'I hope your children are well.' His words were banal because really her offspring had been difficult and he wasn't particularly interested in their health or anything else for that matter. But still it seemed at that moment some conversation was required as her gaze intensified.

'They are indeed, Mr Moreland. Barbara was eighteen last week, if you can believe it. I certainly cannot as it only seems like yesterday that she was born, but she has turned into such a beauty that people everywhere…'

Oliver let her voice blur into the background. The girl in white was near him now, he could see the embroidery in her gown and the gold that threaded through her hair. He wished she might turn towards him so that he could properly observe her face, but Alberton had whisked her off in the opposite direction and she was swallowed up by a sea of people.

Further afield Lady Susan Drummond and Mrs Cecelia Furness were trying to catch his attention, two women whom he had also once bedded. Both had found new husbands and for that he was grateful. He wished he could simply leave and find entertainment that was more to his style, but he had promised his aunt that he would be here and he generally tried to keep his word as far as she was concerned. His mother's sister was in temperament as different as chalk and cheese, her sunny affability the polar opposite of her sister's melancholy. Julia had never had children, but had attached herself most firmly to him and Phillip.

Josephine was still speaking of her daughter and a shiver of horror ran up Oliver's spine. Was she spinning this long monologue to try to interest him in the girl? God, he believed that that was what she was doing and smiled accordingly, but when the dance finally ended he escorted her back to where she had found him and excused himself promptly.

He needed to get out of the room, he thought, the warmth and the expectations suddenly excessive and draining. Already he could see others ready to pounce upon him with their hopes and expectations and so he headed for the French doors at the far end of the salon, not looking at anyone as he went.

Outside it was cooler, a long, enclosed glass room sheltering him from the weather and a good deal of greenery in pots making the place a calm oasis. Breathing in, he closed his eyes.

'You could not bear it, either?'

A voice from behind made him turn, and the girl in white was standing near the tallest potted tree, a drink in hand as she gazed out on to the stormy night.

In this setting she looked untouchable and serene, the debutante from inside swallowed up by a girl who was much more sure of herself.

'I seldom last long at this sort of thing.' He tried to keep the sting from his reply.

'Because you prefer something different entirely?'

As she sipped at the drink he saw dimples appearing in her cheeks.

'You know of my alarming reputation, then, Miss Barrington-Hall?' It was no use beating around the bush, for the girl looked like someone who would appreciate directness.

'Barely. I have just arrived in London, but you do not strike me as a man overly comfortable within polite society.'

'With such instincts you will do well here, I think.'

He could hear the humour in his voice as he said it, but she frowned.

'"Well" in the manner of procuring a husband with an elevated title who can support me in the way I am accustomed to for the rest of my life?'

He heard the irritation easily and finished his explanation.

'I was thinking "well" in the way of becoming an Original. I imagine it to simply be your choice.'

'You allow the feminine sex too much power, sir. London is not a place where women hold much of that, I am afraid.'

'You are from the country, then?'

'I am and I much prefer it to the city.'

Again he smiled. It was not often that he talked to women like this and one who gave no impression at all of wanting any sort of intimacy from him, her aloofness becoming both a challenge and a question.

'The Barrington-Halls are a well-respected family.' Perhaps if he appealed to her connections she might be more forthcoming.

'They are.'

'A family, I suspect, who put much stock in the way of rules and propriety.'

'Which suits me completely, sir.'

'I have heard you enjoy rules?'

'Just as I have heard that you do not.'

'An impasse, then. Perhaps I could persuade you to take another point of view?'

'But why would I want to do that, Mr Moreland, when safety in society lies in the strict observance of manners?'

She raised her glass at him then and simply disappeared through another set of French doors he had not noticed behind her, one moment there and then gone. Like the trickery on show at a country fair, the impression startlingly theatrical.

Intriguing and titillating. Had she meant for it to be so?

He did not want to follow her for she had dismissed him quite directly, and if Oliver knew the ways of one thing, it was the ways of women.

She had been surprising, this mysterious girl with her unusual green eyes and floating white dress, so he would be, too. Already his mind was beginning to work with a plan.

It was him. She had known that it was when she had seen him up close on the dance floor, the man who had rescued her and Mama from a night on the streets all those years before. He'd barely changed—hardened, perhaps, and filled out—but they were the same dark blue eyes that had watched her before, calculating strategy, deciding on what to do.

He was taller than she remembered him and one hand was bedecked with rings. She had looked for the thin gold band of her father's among them, but of course he would not have worn something so small nor would his taste have run to something so insignificant.

He had been out there in the isolation of the greenery room for a reason, she could see that in his eyes. Escape, if she might name it, as before he had realised that she was there his hand had run up and down his left side as though it pained him.

She'd always noticed detail because her mother had been so very poor at reading signals. A much-practised expertise, she supposed, and one she hid from others.

What was it he had said to her about being an Original? That it was her choice? That she could be exactly who she wanted to be?

She frowned, for what was the chance of that? A chicken did not court the notice of foxes if it hoped to survive for any length of time and Esther was sensible enough to know that there was much in her that should remain hidden. No, Mr Oliver Moreland was a man to be avoided at all costs, a rule-breaker who was undisciplined in his personal life and dangerous because of it.

Lord Alberton found her within a few seconds of re-entering the main room, attaching himself to her side with an easy chatter. Mr Moreland's words had been complicated and veiled. Alberton's were simple and undemanding and made her feel as if she belonged here in this room with all the others, a straightforward, unworldly girl who had not seen too much. A debutante who fitted into the narrow definitions of all that was expected of one.

She placed her wine glass on a tray as she walked with Lord Alberton, declining the next offering. The shock of recognising Oliver Moreland was still with her, still humming below her outward appearance, still making her swallow as she found a breath.

'Would you like some air, Miss Barrington-Hall? I know of a place that is much more private.' He glanced towards the greenery room she had just left and she shook her head.

'I think I am hungry, Lord Alberton, and I noticed some tables with food just over there.'

'Of course.'

He tucked her hand into the crook of his arm as he led her off and she allowed him to do so.

Oliver saw her smiling at Alberton, her hand across his arm, the girl he had spoken with reverting back to society debutante Miss Esther Barrington-Hall. She suited her name because the biblical meaning of Esther was secret or hidden, and instinct told him that was exactly what she was.

He wished he might have spoken longer with her, he wished he could have asked her to dance, but with the aunt and uncle and the cousins present he knew there to be little chance of that. Refusing the offer of another drink by a passing servant, he walked over to Frederick, who was leaning against a pillar to one side of the room and watching the dancers.

'I wondered where you were, Oliver. I thought you had indeed exited to that warm carriage you spoke of before. Julia was here a moment ago, asking after you.'

'I needed some air.' He said nothing of Miss Esther Barrington-Hall, which was surprising, but for some reason he did not wish his friend to know that he had talked with her.

He could see her now, surrounded by people over where a few tables of food were laid out. The two girl cousins were on either side of her like sentries, though there was an outer circle of hopeful young swains in attendance, too, Alberton included. The blonde in her hair caught the light of the chandeliers to form a sort of halo above her, the white in her dress completing the effect.

So her first foray into society was proving a success, the beautiful young niece of two of its prominent members rising through milk like cream. He'd have liked to walk through the throngs to speak again with her, but his reputation could only harm such a debut and he knew he should keep away.

His aunt was beside him now and she pulled him over to a quieter portion of the salon.

'You look pensive?'

'Tired more like, Julia. I've had a few late nights recently.'

'She is beautiful, isn't she?'

His hope of his glances having escaped his aunt's notice withered and he did not do her the disservice of pretending to not know of whom she spoke.

'I imagine Miss Esther Barrington Hall will be married before she knows it, for she is surrounded by eligible and interested suitors.'

'I knew her mother once and Alexandra was almost as attractive as her daughter.'

'What happened to her?'

'She died some years ago. An illness of the stomach, I think it was said, though there was talk of other things and I wondered…' She didn't go on.

'Wondered what?'

'Oh, nothing. She was a woman who was different, a woman who did not enjoy the tight rules so adhered to by society, a free spirit if you like, who might have done better had she married a different man.'

'Whom did she marry?'

'Lord Duggan's younger brother. Esther's father. A stickler for the mundane and one who liked his wine overmuch.'

'He was a drunk?'

'The Barrington-Halls would not call him that, I suspect. He died before his wife did and I lost touch with Alexandra afterwards. Rumour had it she left town and found a suitable residence in the country with her small daughter and it was not until years later that the young Miss Esther returned to the Duggan fold, but without her mama. She was about thirteen or fourteen, if I remember it right, and rather a quiet child. Certainly she showed none of the promise that she does here tonight, for she was thin and withdrawn. The colour of her eyes is particularly unusual, would you not say?'

'I do not know.'

'They are a vibrant and clear green and unlike any

others I have observed. Was it so difficult to see her, then, out among the greenery?'

He smiled at that because he should have caught her meaning a sentence or so back.

'Don't worry. No one else saw you. I made sure of it by stationing myself before the first door leading into the room and waiting until she left.'

'Then I thank you for doing so.'

'She sounded quite formidable, if I might make my opinion known. She sounded most unlike the girl we see now. I wonder why she felt safe to let you observe who she truly was?'

'Julia…?'

'Yes.'

'Come and dance with me, for I have not seen you on the floor all evening and a bit of exercise might help you forget these suppositions that have no basis in truth at all.'

He was dancing with an older woman now and they looked comfortable together. Esther wondered what it must be like to partner a man like that in a dance, with all his darkness and his beauty. A troubled man. A man who had not made the best choices in life by all accounts. A man who was rich in assets, but poor in morals. She bet he drank a lot, too, though she had not seen him take more than one glass all evening.

Horror streaked inside Esther

Why would she be watching him? Was she becoming like her mother with her unwise regard for damaged and dangerous men? She shook her head slightly. It was only that the history they shared held a certain poignancy, a trail back to a difficult time in her life and a kindness on his behalf that she had never forgotten. He had always been her handsome knight in shining armour.

She had questioned if she might see him again, his face burned into her memory in an exactness. She wondered what might have happened if he had not stopped and taken them to Camden Town in the middle of that freezing night when everything had looked so bleak.

A year later her mother would be dead.

The colour and whirl of so many people in this ballroom was disorientating. Mr Moreland had left the dance floor now and was walking with another man towards the door. He moved in the way of a man who knew exactly who he was.

Was he leaving?

Did she want him to?

Lord Alberton at her side was relating to her his love of horses and horse racing. She schooled her face into interest even as she looked across his shoulder at the departing form of Oliver Moreland.

He would not ask her for a dance. He would not talk to her again. He'd probably already forgotten their strange conversation tonight. He had not recognised her at all.

She had been plainer at twelve, she supposed, and beset by worry. Esther could barely remember when she and her mother had partaken of a full meal or had a bed for the night that was warm, comfortable and safe. The effort of keeping Alexandra living till the next day had worn Esther down, the alcohol, the laudanum, the night-time assignations with men who were frightening and common.

Each morning she had tried to persuade Alexandra to return to the family that her mother often mentioned in Kent, but by night-time the desperation of addiction had blackened her mother's soul again and all Esther could do was retire into a corner out of the way and try to watch over her.

In retrospect it had been a lucky thing that she looked about nine and not twelve. Had she been any prettier or more developed those who crawled around her mother might have noticed her and God knew what that could have led to.

'Did you have horses when you were a girl, Miss Barrington-Hall? I feel I have been taking up too much of the conversation and would be interested to hear of your particular and personal stories.'

The question jolted her right back into the present. 'We did, Lord Alberton, but none quite so fine as the ones you describe.'

It was so easy to lie sometimes, the second nature of a child brought up on the hard streets of desperation.

'But I imagine you loved your horses? My sister certainly adored anything with four legs.'

Esther nodded. She had a far greater personal knowledge of rats, bedbugs and cockroaches than horses, and those things she certainly had not adored.

'I'd like to show you some of the finer specimens in my stables. Benjamin and any of your cousins would be welcome to come, too, and we could make an occasion of it. The family estate, Grafton Manor, is just outside Barnet, and my mother and father reside there. Perhaps you might all join us for a house party running over a few days? We could easily arrange it.'

His face was sunny and hopeful and because of it Esther nodded. He was a good man, Lord Alberton, and one whom she could see the other young ladies around them glance at often. A good man who deserved a bride without the hidden secrets she was full of, a simple man who would not find complications attractive. When he talked every word was threaded with the manners and comportment of entitlement, the expectation that everyone he met would have had an upbringing on a par with his own, the horses, the stables, the ease of a life that was not marred by bad choices and poor selections. With him very little must have fallen out of place and she could imagine he might not have much patience with those who had problems.

'A house party sounds lovely and I know that Charlotte in particular would enjoy it, for out of all of us she is the one who loves horses the most.'

Her aunt and uncle had now joined them and so had a few of their friends, so it was a happy party who went through together to the final supper when it was called.

'You have made such an impression, my love.' Her aunt squeezed her hand in relief. 'I thought, of course, that you would, but society is often fickle and one never knows how one will be received. Lord Alberton looks most enamoured with you, as do many other of the sons of those well placed here.'

Esther was glad she had not failed her aunt, but as she walked with her family she watched carefully for any sight of the enigmatic Oliver Moreland.

Chapter Two

Charlotte and Sarah collapsed on her bed the next morning, each of them eager to hear a recount of the previous evening.

Esther had slept badly, her night full of fretful dreams about her mother, and the face of Mr Oliver Moreland had appeared in every one of them. A beautiful, complex and dangerous man reaching out from her past, the chaos of before suddenly entangled with her present and she did not like it.

'Lord Alberton appeared most taken by you, Esther, and everyone says he is charming and wealthy. He is newly back from a journey to the Americas so I imagine he must be an interesting conversationalist as well.'

'He does speak of horses quite a bit.'

'That's because he runs a stable that is by all accounts one of the most magnificent in the land. How I would love to see that.'

Charlotte said this in a way that made Esther smile.

'Well, as fate has it you are in luck. He has invited

us all to visit the Beaumont estate, Grafton Manor, sometime soon. He was most insistent we take up the invitation as a family.'

'The whole lot of us?' Sarah asked this, her eyes alight.

'Every cousin is how he put it and he hopes to make it a house party with other guests as well running over a few days.'

Sarah clapped. 'Jeremy will love you for this and even Aiden will be delighted, though he won't show it.'

'Aiden is young, Sarah, and a little bit stupid.' This was from Charlotte. 'As we are older and far more sensible we realise the value of such an invitation. Lord Alberton is most handsome, by the way, with his blond hair, dark eyes and the Beaumont bone structure.'

'Not as handsome as Oliver Moreland, though,' her sister returned. 'Did you see the way his appearance made veritable waves in the ballroom last night? Every lady there wished he might look at her and ask her to dance.'

'I hardly think Aunt Mary would have thought anything of the sort,' Esther chimed in. 'Hasn't he a terrible reputation?'

Sarah considered the question before answering. 'Well, I've never heard anything truly ghastly about him and most of the women he has escorted seem to remain friends. If he was an ogre, I am sure they would not. Penelope Churchill, for example, says her aunt speaks highly of him, though perhaps it is because she is a lady who is almost a widow and one who seeks out his company.'

'Almost a widow?' Esther was fascinated. 'How can one be that?'

'Her husband has been in India for years and so I suppose there is a case to be made. Mr Moreland takes her to some of the society functions, though there has never been a hint of impropriety publicly.'

'Well, in him that is rich.'

Charlotte enunciated the words with a great dollop of censure. 'Remember Gwen Keene? She thought he loved her and turned down a proposal from Lord Weatherby, who then ran away to Gretna Green with her best friend, Larissa Kepple, the very next week. She would say Oliver Moreland is a bounder and a cad.'

'But what she wouldn't say, of course, is that she got it all wrong and laid an intent in Mr Moreland's heart that was never there in the first place.' Sarah loved a debate. Esther could see delight in her hazel eyes. 'She might even say that she was beyond foolish, if she were more truthful, and that she needed to choose her friends with greater care.'

Esther listened with interest. The world of the *ton* was like a sticky spider's web, all unvoiced supposition and implied conclusions.

Sarah was lying next to her now, busy fingers making tiny plaits in her long dark hair, plaits that fell apart almost immediately. 'You did look beautiful last night, though, Esther. I heard people say it everywhere I went and I am glad it was such a success for you. Mama could not have been more pleased, of course, and she attributed her own sense of what suited you dress-wise to be a major factor.'

'Well, all the dresses in the world that she has chosen for us did not make the same impression, so I am certain it is more than just a gown, Sarah. Men across the room were eulogising on the colour of your eyes all night, dear Cousin.' Charlotte said this with feeling as Sarah began to laugh. 'I heard it said they were like emeralds or water running across seagrass and even the colour of the newly budding oak leaves in the springtime. Certainly no one has ever been quite so forthcoming on the colour of our eyes, Sarah. Hazel eyes have not the same allure as a mysterious green.'

'We will have our day, too, Charlotte. Surely there was someone at the ball whom you fancied.'

Charlotte threw a pillow at her sister and a small flurry of feathers flew into the air. 'No one, and I shall never marry until I fall desperately and hopelessly in love. I only pray the man has a stable as well stocked as Lord Alberton's.' She began to pick up the feathers even as she said this, for Charlotte hated mess in any form at all. 'Aiden looked to be enjoying the dance he had with you, Esther. He seemed to be putting a lot of effort into his steps.'

'He was, although I doubt I could claim the same enjoyment for my feet, for he stood on them numerous times.'

They all fell back into giggles and Esther knew that a great deal of her happiness was due to these two cousins who had welcomed her into their family right from the start. Charlotte was only six months older than she was and Sarah a year and a half, but she had never felt excluded in their circle. Esther knew Aunt Mary and Uncle Thomas had told them something of her former circumstances just to make sense of her arrival, but they certainly did not know all of it and for that she was glad. She never saw shadows in their eyes, nor pity, and she could not have abided either.

At one o'clock in the afternoon the family was gathered in the green salon, a room with wide windows overlooking St James's Square and presently filled with floral arrangements sent after the night's entertainment. Many of them were addressed to Esther.

She did not even recognise the names on some of the bouquets, though the biggest one by far proudly sported Lord Alberton's message.

With my best regards,
Alberton

'You seem to have made an impression, Esther,' her uncle quipped. 'At least the flower sellers of London town will be relieved you have come to their city.'

'I can't even imagine who would want to spend so much money on a bouquet that is stuffed in with all the others so that it can hardly be seen. It seems such an awful waste, in my opinion, given that every bloom will die in a week.'

Aiden made this comment and his father frowned.

'You wait, my boy. One day you will meet a

woman who makes your heart flutter and your world will be changed and all for the better. Then you, too, shall be sending flowers to try to catch the young lady's attention and interest.'

Aunt Mary laughed as she ran her hands across some of the blooms on the table in the middle of the room.

'This one in particular has caught my fancy. No name and an unusual message. I wonder who can have sent it.'

Esther hadn't seen this arrangement, tucked as it was behind the larger bunches, but the simplicity of a dozen white roses mixed in with the soft green, fuzzy leaves of sage was unusual. The smell of mint was strong as she walked over to look, though as she turned over the card her heart stopped.

An Original.

That was all that it said, but she absolutely knew whom it was from.

'It is unsigned, which is most odd.' There was a note in Aunt Mary's voice that was worrying. Charlotte had wandered over now, too, and made much of observing the message.

'The sender thinks Esther is an Original, Mama, and of course he is right. I applaud his taste and his certainty as the bouquet hints of the gown she wore and of the colour of her eyes. A clever man. A cultured man. A suitor who is neither common nor conventional, I would wager. A man who does not wish to be identified, either. Does anyone have any ideas as to who it might be?'

Such a query in this family was like opening the door to loud opinion, though Benjamin got in first.

'Not Alberton, I think, for his offering was at the other end of the scale. Gaudy and tasteless.'

Sarah laughed, as did Aiden. Aunt Mary, however, looked displeased.

'Who else did you dance with, Esther?' This came from Jeremy, who was draped across the *chaise longue* by the window and looking much the worse for wear after his late night.

'Uncle Thomas,' she returned, and more laughter ensued.

'Your uncle does not have the sensitivity to send such an arrangement. His offerings to me when we first met were much more in the style of those from Lord Alberton.'

'What of Hemmingworth? You danced with him, did you not?' Jeremy persisted in his queries.

'Once, but we hardly spoke.'

'Not a talker, Charles Smythe, I am afraid, but he's a very good fisherman. No wonder he did not converse much, Esther.'

'He doesn't sound like the culprit, then,' Aiden mused.

'The culprit,' her aunt spluttered. 'I will have you know, Aiden Barrington-Hall, that it is kindness that motivates young men of good breeding to send flowers to a lady who has caught their eye. He is hardly to be chastised.'

'What of that bunch, then?' Her youngest cousin pointed to a medium-sized bouquet of purple, pink and orange flowers that clashed in a way that was not pleasant. 'Could that not be thought of as criminal?'

All joviality was cut short by the sound of the door knocker and Esther felt her heartbeat quicken. Would Mr Moreland come here to call on her and her family? She smoothed down her skirt and tidied her hair, sitting up just a little bit straighter.

'Lord Alberton, my lord.' The butler gave the name and the visitor walked in, his eyes finding hers before the second step.

'I see you have received my flowers, Miss Barrington-Hall, among many others.'

To give him credit the words were brave in front of her whole family and the many other bouquets scattered on every flat surface in the room.

'Thank you, my lord, I did and they are lovely.'

Aiden and Jeremy stood now and excused themselves and Esther saw in their expressions identical looks of astonishment and hilarity. She was glad when they left and glad, too, that Benjamin had stayed for he might at least provide some sort of buffer to Lord Alberton's obvious regard for her.

The budding white roses amid the green bunch of sage seemed to scoff at her from their place on the top of the table.

An Original.

She could not believe that Mr Moreland would have sent her such a gift.

'It was a wonderful occasion last night.' Her suitor

sat down beside her, leaving the proper amount of room between them on the sofa.

'Indeed it was.' Aunt Mary could always be counted upon to cover awkward silences. 'The food was more than ample and most delicious. The Creightons outdid themselves this year and I suppose the revelry went on till the early hours of this morning?'

Lord Alberton frowned. 'I am not sure, Lady Duggan, for I left very soon after you did.'

'A wise choice,' Ben interjected. 'Aiden and Jeremy were not home until just a few hours ago. I imagine we won't see them now for the rest of the day.'

'Will you take tea with us, Lord Alberton?' her aunt asked, and he nodded.

Sarah on the other side of the room looked slightly pained as if the intrusion of someone other than family in their midst was a large bother, but Charlotte appeared thrilled to have him here, no doubt hoping that the talk might turn to that of horses. Esther on her part resolved to be polite to a man who had been more than generous towards her. When the topic changed to that of the forthcoming house party he had mentioned last night, she tried to appear as thrilled as the rest of her family seemed to be.

He should not have sent the damned flowers, he knew he should not have, yet some wild foolish whim had had him scurrying off to a flower seller and placing his order.

The note was another mistake. His name would have been ample, but instead he had concocted an obscure reference to their brief chat which in retrospect he felt unwise.

He'd never sent flowers to any woman before and was amazed at his want to do so to one who, by her own admission, would hardly welcome the advances of a suitor who'd broken most of the rules in a society she so steadfastly stood by.

But that was the crux of it. Esther Barrington-Hall was everything he had always shied away from—the fact that he now was not shying away floored him. He had no chance of meeting her again, for to call on her at home would only arouse question and he hadn't the desire to be interrogated by Lord and Lady Duggan and their large family as to his intentions.

No. Miss Barrington-Hall was out of bounds to a man like him and if she had even an inkling of his dreams last night she would be running for the hills and away as fast as she could go.

His dreams. Explicit and shocking, the elegant and innocent young Miss Barrington-Hall naked beneath him as he showed her sensual things he'd learnt over the years.

'God.'

He sat down on his bed and tried to take stock of where he was and to find some way out of the complications. He'd go riding and blow out some of the cobwebs, that was what he would do. The severe cold would put most people off visiting Hyde Park and he needed some fresh air and quiet.

* * *

'There was an accident in Hyde Park today. Mr Moreland fell from his horse and has hurt himself, it seems.'

Aunt Mary said this as Esther came down to the dinner table with Charlotte and Sarah. The boys were not joining them tonight and Uncle Thomas was at a meeting.

'My goodness.' Charlotte spoke first. 'Is he badly hurt?'

'He has been taken home to his town house in Westminster. Nothing seems broken by all accounts, but people said his horse was suddenly uncontrollable as he galloped off the track on Rotten Row, his stallion the colour of midnight and his steed's breath steaming in the cold. According to those who observed the accident his friend Mr Michael Tomlinson was also there.'

Esther felt the shock of his accident echo down the length and breadth of her body.

'Does Mr Moreland have family?' she felt compelled to ask.

'An aunt, only. He is estranged from his brother, the Earl of Elmsworth, and his father died quite a few years ago. A fractured family and a sad one indeed, but I suppose it is a situation he has brought on to himself with his wildness. If one breaks rules with such impunity, one must also suffer the consequences.'

Like her mother had. A further horror juddered through her.

'His friends, no doubt, will rally about him,' Sarah said, and Esther looked up.

'Does a man like that have many?' She tried to place censure in the query.

'He does. More than his brother, at least, who is rumoured to be an arrogant fellow. They fell out completely a year or so back and the Earl is almost never in London, which is probably a relief to the society matrons who would have to juggle invites if they were both in town.' She giggled to herself. 'Oliver Moreland would undoubtedly win that tangle given that he is unmarried.'

'Your knowledge of gossip never ceases to amaze me, Sarah. Perhaps you should spend less time reading the broadsheets and listening to chatter and more time identifying an appropriate young man at whom you might set your cap.'

Her aunt's rebuke was so familiar her cousin merely laughed.

'When I find the one I shall let you know, Mama, but at the moment I am enjoying the freedom of the Season.'

'Well, do not leave it too long. You are almost twenty-one, my dear, and the world will not be kind to a woman with too many more years under her belt.'

And there it was again, Esther thought, that talk of a small window of opportunity for women to make something of themselves by marrying well. Yet her mother had married well and look what had happened to her.

If she encouraged Lord Alberton, she would no doubt score a husband of good manners and a careful social presence. He would never take to the drink like her father had or make it his business to sleep with every woman in London. He was a wealthy man and a solid one, a man whom she might trust to do the right thing in the face of temptation.

Yet why did she not dream of him?

Why had Oliver Moreland's face inhabited her thoughts last night? Burying that reflection, she raced on to another.

There was to be a ball tomorrow evening at the home of Lord and Lady Keegan and they had all been invited. Her aunt had said that Lady Keegan was one of the most prominent hosts in London and that her soirées were always a sought-after invitation.

Oliver Moreland would not be there, of course, after his awful accident, but that was a good thing. Without the pressure of looking around for him Esther would be able to better concentrate on Lord Alberton and find his measure with more certainty. She knew Alberton would be attending because he had told her so this afternoon.

Esther had taken the green-and-white bouquet up to her room earlier and placed it on the table beside her bed, looking at the card more often than she would have liked to admit. Alberton's flowers were there, too, on the far mantel, but more out of expectation than any considered want. She'd simply put them there and had barely glanced at them since. All the other floral gifts were still in the downstairs salon. Perhaps Aiden had been right in his stated disdain for suitors sending such expensive offerings, which were then abandoned to wither and die with barely a backward glance.

She wondered where Oliver Moreland would be at this exact moment, seven o'clock and the winter darkness well upon them.

Would he be feeling better or did he lurk in the land of the barely living, a doctor attending him with a nervous brow and a clear knowledge of what such alarming symptoms might entail? Was the relative her aunt had spoken of there with him? Or was he alone in his ailment, the gossip of the *ton* swirling in both horror and eager malevolence to find out what might happen next to the dissolute and wild younger brother of the arrogant Earl of Elmsworth?

'You seem distracted tonight, Esther,' Aunt Mary said, 'for I have asked you twice whether you would like some wine with your dinner?'

'I am sorry, Aunt, and, no, I will have the lemonade, thank you.'

Aunt Mary gestured to the footman, who immediately poured the drink in her glass. Then her aunt began to speak again. 'It is just as well it was such a horrid day today as Hyde Park would have been mercifully empty. Imagine if Mr Moreland's undisciplined horse had run into a phaeton full of people and the damage that would have done.'

'Did he lose control of his steed?' Charlotte asked.

'Well, that is the strange thing. Word has it that there was a loud noise just before the stallion took off and Moreland was getting him under management when he was brushed up against a fence.'

'Did the horse survive, Mama?'

'Fortunately the stallion walked away unhurt. It was only the rider who was damaged.'

'What was the noise, do you think?' Esther could not help but ask.

'A branch falling in the storm, perhaps, or a stone turned up from the hooves of the animal. Presumably Mr Moreland can add his opinion of the accident when he recovers.'

Esther was glad her aunt said *when* and not *if.*

'Your father should hear more about the whole unfortunate incident tonight at his meeting, for I am sure he will be, as usual, the talk of the *ton*. On another matter, Lady Beaumont sent a letter over this afternoon with an invitation to a house party at Barnet. It will be in a month so we must make sure we have everything we need, for the Beaumonts were very hopeful our entire family could be in attendance.'

Things seemed to be moving on at a speed Esther felt to be uncomfortably fast. She had been to one society outing and already her name was becoming linked to Lord Alberton. She did not even know his full given name, for goodness' sake, and she had no idea at all on his opinions about the things that mattered most to her. In fact, the only conversation last night that had been interesting was the one with Oliver Moreland in the long room beyond the French doors.

Stop thinking of him, she chastised herself, and helped herself to a generous portion of the steaming hot chicken pie.

* * *

Oliver had a headache that defied description, blood thumping in his ears and a sort of fatigue that was making him feel sick.

God. Someone had shot at either Michael or him, he was sure of it, shot at them in the confines of a well-used public park in the middle of the afternoon.

Frederick sat in a chair beside him in the library of his town house, the candles lit and the rain outside making itself known. Barrett Brooker was on the *chaise longue* by the fire.

'Are you sure you should be having another brandy, Oliver? Didn't the doctor say to abstain?' Freddie had always been a stickler for the advice of physicians.

'Anyone with a headache such as I have deserves a brandy.'

'Sleep is probably a more appropriate remedy, but then the physician doesn't have a clue as to what actually happened to you so maybe a strong drink works just as well.' Frederick sounded plain irritated now.

'You're sure it was a shot?' Barrett's eyes were golden in this light, like a hawk about to pounce on its prey. Oliver knew he had been dabbling in espionage for a few years and was glad his friend was here.

'I am.'

'I'll go and look around the area tomorrow, then, and see if I can find the bullet.'

'I'll help you.' Freddie's offer was enthusiastic.

'No. It's better if I go alone as we don't want any more talk flying around than is there already. There might be clues left and at least the scene won't be being trampled over with this sort of deluge. Did Michael have any idea as to who it could be?'

'None. Though working in Whitechapel as he does, he has collected enemies.'

Freddie looked up. 'What about you? You are often there, too.'

Oliver shrugged and took another large sip of the brandy he held, but only because he could not spit out the words that boiled inside him.

Could it be his brother who had done this, trying to finish a job he had started a year ago? Even at close range and with the full amount of surprise on his side, Phillip had missed last time, so a moving target in driving rain would have been more than impossible for him.

The thought of another run-in with a member of his family simply exhausted him, though he knew there were others, too, in Whitechapel who would have liked him dead. He had partnered Michael long enough at St Mary's to know he had made his own enemies in the process.

God. He just wanted things simple, though the word made him smile. It was probably too late for that after taking on the poorhouses in the brutal streets of east London, the places where girls and boys as young as five were being sold into prostitution and slavery for a few shillings or less.

The two sides of his life were beginning to collide and fracture, the one who dwelt in society and the other, who walked nameless in the shadows of poverty and deprivation, trying to make a difference.

His thoughts returned to Esther Barrington-Hall

and the way she had looked at him with her brilliant green eyes for all of the few minutes he had had with her in the enclosed glass room.

'Vibrant, clear green eyes, unlike any others I have observed.'

His aunt's words from the Creighton ball came back to him even as a flash from the past did, blinding him with its truth. He knew those eyes because he had seen them before on the child in the carriage on that snowy London street six years before.

He seldom forgot a face and it was just the transition between child- and adulthood that had confused him. Esther Barrington-Hall was that girl and if he knew her through the fog of time she almost certainly would have recognised him, for unlike her he had not changed much at all.

The world spun for a moment and Freddie leapt out of his chair and came towards him.

'Are you all right? Should I get the doctor back again?'

'No.'

Now the headache was only the second of his problems.

'I am fine, really.' He put his brandy down because he needed all the focus he could muster. 'But I think I should go to bed. Can you let yourselves out when you leave?'

Both his friends looked concerned.

'Sleep is the great restorer as you said. I am sure that I will feel better in the morning.'

He left them then, walking taking all of his energy, and once outside he found the wall with his hand and guided himself up the staircase to his room. His left leg was painful.

What the hell had the young Esther been doing on the streets of London at midnight, cowering in a door well? Her mother had been there, too, the sad woman with the split lip. He remembered thinking she was perhaps a drunk, her demeanour one of resignation and defeat.

Alexandra Barrington-Hall, his aunt had said. A free-spirited woman who had married the wrong man. A man who was an alcoholic.

Had Duggan's younger brother abused her? Why had they not stayed with the Barrington-Halls after Esther's father had drunk himself to death? So many questions. He needed to talk to his aunt as soon as possible, but he could not face it tonight.

No, tonight he needed to rest and recuperate. He needed to regain his strength and his wits to do what was required next.

The ring then came to mind—the small gold ring the child had left in the blanket as payment when they exited the carriage. Where the hell would that be? He could not remember the inscription inside, but he knew there had been a date and some initials. He'd try to find the thing tomorrow among his things because it would still be here.

Incredulity layered across shock, and weariness underwrote that. But exhaustion was winning. He needed bed and he needed sleep. Every other problem would just have to wait in a queue until the morrow.

Chapter Three

Esther was not looking forward to tonight's outing. Granted, her dress and hair were as beautiful as they had felt at the Creightons' ball, but she felt a certain heaviness that she was having trouble shifting.

Lord Alberton would be there, of course, with his charm and his smiles and his endless conversation about horses and stables and America. He would be polite and genuine and mannerly, a well-bred lord of the *ton* who was cultured, sophisticated and polished. He would compliment her effusively, she was sure he would, and then they would dance the allowed number of dances. He would probably take her into supper when it was called and all around people's voices would be whispering about that which was so plain in front of their eyes.

A new couple, a wonderful and well-matched pair.

But she did not wish to be partnered with someone so quickly, the *ton's* penchant to marry its young off before they had had the chance to sample other fare a worrying thing.

She had asked her aunt the other day about how fast her own parents had wed and Aunt Mary had smiled as she'd answered 'within a few weeks, my dear', as if a love match had been wielded from mere moments and seconds, no reckoning at all given as to how awfully it had actually turned out.

And that was the crux of it. Esther did not want a marriage like her mother's. She did not wish to marry a man whom she might lose respect for or, worse, who might make her lose respect for herself, for without getting to know someone properly there was every chance that would happen.

She wanted what she saw in Aunt Mary and Uncle Thomas, a warm, close friendship tinged with true admiration and permanency because a solid centre made it easier for everyone, the whole family flourishing under a tutelage of virtue and integrity. As she had, too, the young girl who had come to this house all those years ago transformed under their kindness, even though it had not been easy…

She let that thought go and concentrated on the here and now. The silk of her dress was a light airy blue and her hair had been curled and threaded with the same coloured ribbons. She wore a pearl necklace at her throat, one Aunt Mary had given her on her birthday last year, wrought in fine gold and with a clasp of diamonds.

But still she felt tense.

There had been no more talk of the accident in Hyde Park, no awful news of an untimely death and even Uncle Thomas had told Charlotte that from what he could deduce Mr Moreland's mishap would probably see him up and about before the week's end.

People had accidents on horses all the time, didn't they? Falls, kicks, bites were a common risk of keeping a stable, after all, and she could not imagine Oliver Moreland to favour a gentle ride. If she kept her ears open, she would undoubtedly hear more about how he fared tonight and she meant to do just that.

An hour later amid the crowd and on the arm of Lord Alberton, Esther had some answers at least. Lord Alberton's given name was Henry and Mr Moreland was not at death's door.

'Frederick Bronson was at White's late last night, though he was fairly tight-lipped about Oliver Moreland's condition. Moreland is a good rider, I will give him that, and I know the horse he was on, too, a fine specimen whom I'd like to get my hands on. Perhaps the weather had an effect on the track or on the vegetation and made it slippery or uneven for there was a crack, by all accounts, and the horse veered wildly, throwing Moreland into a fence on the side of the path. He did walk away afterwards, and Michael Tomlinson escorted him home, so I am sure we will see him back in society before too long.'

Benjamin stood beside them, listening to Alberton's long account of the accident and then giving his own opinion on the matter.

'He is like a cat with nine lives. There was talk of a much worse injury last year, if you remember.'

'When he disappeared completely for a few

months? An accident to the ribs, wasn't it? I'd forgotten about that.'

'The details never came out. If Moreland has one
thing going for him, it is a set of loyal friends. They
never uttered a word.'

Such news interested Esther as she recalled him
rubbing his left side on the balcony and stretching in
a way that told of great pain. But Ben had changed the
subject now to that of the forthcoming house party.

'My family are looking forward to a tour of your
stables, Henry. It's been an age since I was up there.
Charlotte, my youngest sister, in particular is horse
mad and speaks of your invitation constantly.'

'A girl after my own heart, then.' Alberton chuckled and Esther saw him glance in the direction of her
cousin, who was standing speaking to a group of her
friends and looking most fetching.

'Whereas Esther is simply afraid of anything larger
than a cat. It's been a family joke for years.'

Benjamin began to laugh and she coloured slightly,
remembering telling Alberton that she adored horses
just a few days before, though if Lord Alberton recalled
her words he gave no sign at all of having done so.

'We will find you a docile mare to ride, Miss
Barrington-Hall, for your outings when you come
up to Grafton Manor. Certainly I have nothing in
my stable as wild as Moreland's steed.'

'Just as well,' her cousin interjected. 'Did you see
any fine horseflesh in America, Henry, when you
were there? I'd meant to ask.'

Esther looked around the room because she knew

that such a question would lead to a long and detailed answer on Alberton's behalf.

Her uncle smiled at her from across a small distance and further afield she saw her cousin Sarah speaking with her friends. To the other side of the room Aunt Mary was conversing with the same woman that Mr Moreland had been dancing with the other night at the Creighton ball. Excusing herself, she walked over to join them.

'Ahh, Esther, I would like you to meet an old school friend of mine, Miss Julia Buckley. Julia, this is my niece, Miss Esther Barrington-Hall, and it is her first Season here in London.'

The other woman smiled.

'I am most gratified to be introduced finally, my dear, and I have heard only good things about you. Your aunt must be very proud.'

'Oh, I can assure you I am, Julia.' Aunt Mary's words held warmth.

'Your mother, Alexandra, was a friend of mine once, a friend whom I lost touch with all those years ago, and I was sorry to hear of her untimely passing.'

Esther saw that Julia Buckley was genuinely sad. Aunt Mary had spoken of her mother with her from time to time, but there were large missing pieces that her aunt had no want to recall. Esther did know her mother had never felt close to the Barrington-Hall family and had, for a number of years, insisted Esther be known as Esther Hall instead. She also had no idea what her father might have thought of all this because he had died soon after she turned five and any hazy memory of him was long lost, save for the smell of strong liquor and cigar smoke that always emanated from him.

'Are you enjoying your time here in society, Miss Barrington-Hall? From all accounts the handsome Beaumont heir is very fond of your company.'

'I am, thank you, and Lord Alberton is a friend.'

She would not admit to more and she was surprised when the woman opposite her began to smile quite widely, her reply nothing like the words Esther might have expected.

'I am glad to hear you are giving yourself time to acclimatise to the ways of the world here. Marriage is a step in life that needs a proper consideration and it is well worth allowing yourself a good period of weeks or months to look around.'

Aunt Mary frowned. 'I am not certain I agree with all you say, Julia. The first Season that a girl has is always the most fruitful and too much looking around decreases one's chance of catching the best worm, so to speak.'

'Like early birds, you mean?' Julia Buckley began to laugh.

'I do.' Her aunt's face was stony, all humour gone, though the unexpected calling out of Mr Moreland's name by the major-domo had everyone turning and Esther's heartbeat quickened dramatically.

Miss Buckley did not look at all pleased. 'Oh, I'd rather hoped that my nephew would not have come tonight after his nasty accident in the park. I do pray that he is up to such an evening.'

So they were related, this woman and Oliver Moreland, and Julia Buckley appeared worried as she turned to watch him.

He came into the room in the company of the same man Esther had seen him with at the Creighton ball. Tonight he wore navy blue and white, his neckcloth tied high and his hair slicked back. He limped, but only slightly, as if by sheer dint of will he had relegated the accident to the past and no longer wished to dwell upon it.

As they came closer Esther saw him glance at his aunt, but when his eyes met hers she saw no recognition whatsoever. It was as if the flowers she thought he had sent had come from someone else entirely and she wondered if indeed there had been some sort of a mix-up.

When he was swallowed up by a group of people she made her escape, joining Charlotte and two friends on the other side of the room just in case his next intention was to come across to speak with his aunt.

'Mr Moreland does not look too worse for wear, does he?' Wanda Stapleton said and the others shook their heads. 'He simply looks his normal and most beautiful self.'

'And every woman here wishes he would ask her for a dance,' Prudence Hartford whispered, though Charlotte did not look pleased at all.

'If only he would find a wife and settle down, the *ton* would have far less gossip to blather about and we could all just get on with our lives.'

'Whom would he pick, though?' Wanda took up the topic. 'He never goes near any of the debutantes and although he shows interest in some of the older ladies he seldom stays with them for more than a month.'

'Celeste Carlisle lasted longer than that, surely?'

'Yet she left for America ten days after he allegedly walked away. Does that not smack of desperation to you?'

'Josephine Campbell was telling my mother Mr Moreland asked many questions at the Creighton ball about her daughter, Barbara, who turned eighteen recently, and she intimated that she would be thrilled to welcome him into the family.'

Charlotte frowned. 'A difficult proposition given Mrs Campbell and Mr Moreland were lovers not so long ago themselves, do you not think?'

Esther gritted her teeth. She hated all this talk of who was with whom and when because such supposition invariably led to the unmasking of secrets and she was a great believer in people's private business remaining exactly that.

She wished Oliver Moreland had not come. She wished he had not seen her here and looked right through her as if they had never spoken.

He had crossed over to talk with Julia Buckley and even her normally far more sensible aunt looked overcome by his closeness. Others joined them, too, the group growing in size by the second, the laughter emanating from the group astounding.

Oliver Moreland was like some potent beam of

light attracting the moths of society, the women especially hurrying to his side, and not all young women, either. He did not look her way again.

It was for the best he did not, she thought then, because he was a man who lived life, by all accounts, in a far different way than she did. A man who took risks and travelled a path that was not dissimilar to her mother's, the chaos of poor choice walking in each and every footstep that he took.

Lord Balcombe came over to stand beside her and claim his dance and she accompanied him on to the dance floor. As she looked back, though, she caught Oliver Moreland watching her, his dark blue gaze measuring and intent. The spark of shock had her turning away. Even at this distance she could feel a pull, an irresistible and unwelcome tug of the sensual.

Horrified by such a knowledge, she brightened her smile as Balcombe spoke, watching the pleasure on his face blossom in the way of a man who had not expected it. When his hand closed tighter around her own she did not pull away.

Oliver wished he had not come. His realisation that Esther Barrington-Hall was the girl he had picked up all those years ago was colouring his emotions. He did not quite know whether to be glad to see her again or to be angry that she had said nothing of it in the greenery room at the Creightons. Caught between, he thought it was better just to ignore her altogether.

Julia also observed him in a way that was worrying and Lady Duggan, Esther Barrington-Hall's aunt, was plainly disconcerted by his reputation. Moving off from their company, he made a line for the pillars to one side of the room. This world of society had long not been his own and he was more at home in venues of less impossible standards, places where people were easier to understand. There, he could relax, the expectations smaller, the stakes lower, and, adrift in the stupor of strong wine or easy women, time disappeared until the dawn came and he found his way unsteadily home.

Home to one of the lesser well-presented streets in Westminster, an address that might not have been so fashionable, but one that suited him. Close to his clubs, close to Hyde Park and not too far from Whitechapel, where poverty marked a realness into the landscape and the hidden people plied their daily way through desperation.

Men and women lived and died in the confines of small crowded streets and if those in society labelled them as discarded and useless they needed only to spend a day in the community to understand that it was not always so.

There was a heart in the place that was lacking here, an honesty that did not allow for human failings to be judged so narrowly. Not a place for the faint-hearted, but not the haunt of pretence, greed and charade, either. Oliver walked those streets with a far greater knowledge of who he was because his presence was needed and the emptiness that claimed him in all its shades of numbness in society was more distant there.

Esther Barrington-Hall was laughing now at something Balcombe had said and the sound of her happiness was stronger than any drug he'd fallen under the influence of, stronger even than reason, and that indeed was a worrying thing.

He wanted to stride across the dance floor and claim her, take her hand in his and understand what it was that dragged him in, unresisting and bewildered. Swearing under his breath, he shook his head to try to clear such thoughts, and Freddie, joining him now, frowned.

'If you are out of sorts tonight, Oliver, it is entirely of your own doing for you are not well enough to be here and God knows that is the truth.'

'Maybe you are right,' he admitted and took a drink from the tray of a passing waiter. 'Is Brooker here?'

'He has just arrived. It seems he is setting his cap at the Barrington-Hall girl.'

His breath caught. 'Which one?'

'The oldest daughter. Sarah.'

When he looked around there was no sign of his friend.

'Barrett is more than interested by all accounts and he's coming up for twenty-six next month, so…?' Freddie left the question unfinished, but Oliver felt the change in it, the change in all of them, the next part of their lives opening up into something different.

His leg ached as much as his ribs and the headache that he thought gone was back with a vengeance. Freddie was right, he should not have come tonight, but the fact remained that he had wanted to see Esther Barrington-Hall in any way that he could.

Lady Tina Greene had now joined him, the look in her eye one he recognised with a sinking heart.

'I have barely seen you lately, Mr Moreland. You were neither at the Sargesons' the other evening nor at the Carstairs'.'

He made himself smile. 'I have been busy.'

'Busy in the confines of Whitechapel by all accounts? My brother spotted you in the vicinity the other day. He says he heard that you are trying to save souls who do not wish to be saved, but then I am imagining you yourself do not see it in quite that way?'

'You imagine correctly.'

'An exercise of atonement perhaps, then, or penance?'

Anger flushed through him.

'Or maybe just plain Christian charity, Lady Tina.'

The woman looked abashed, and making an excuse, she left them, Oliver resolutely ignoring the smile on Freddie's lips.

'I doubt Tina Greene has much plain Christian charity inside her. Her family is well known for their greed.'

With the music and the dancing and the trilling laughter and chatter around them he felt dislocated and restless. Esther Barrington-Hall glided past them in the arms of Balcombe, her presence even at this distance felt in a small shiver of familiarity. He did not look at her directly, green eyes the last thing in the world he needed to see just at this moment. She would notice his anger and his unrest, he thought, and he did not wish for her to know of the swirling currents that lay inside of him. Usually he was good at hiding his thoughts, but tonight he was finding the charade difficult.

It was partly because of the aches all over his body, but it was mostly because he knew that Esther Barrington-Hall would have recognised him from all those years before and he felt unsettled by that fact. What would she make of such a thing, her secret past with a propensity to be leaked into the public domain and all the ensuing worry that might engender? Would she imagine him her enemy? Would she be leaving a wide berth between them so that a conversation did not eventuate in the shocking truth coming out? Would he be regarded by her as a friend or as a foe? Both positions had their detractions and yet there was no other way.

From this position he saw she was trying her best to simply ignore him, to smile as if she meant it and laugh with the sort of verve that indicated great resolve. He admired her for it because he knew that here in society she was regarded only as the innocent youngest niece of the powerful and honourable Lord and Lady Duggan. He wondered how much even her aunt and uncle had known of Esther's mother's proclivity for things that were dangerous to both her and her daughter.

Barrett Brooker had joined them now and he

looked distracted, his glance travelling around the room and back again.

'If it is Sarah Barrington-Hall you are looking for, she was over in that corner a few seconds ago.'

His friend smiled broadly. 'Freddie has been talking to you, I see. I wondered how long it would take.'

'He is of the opinion change is around the corner for all of us.' Oliver couldn't help laughing as he said this.

'Perhaps he is right. I'm thinking of leaving London altogether and living in the country.'

'At Sanderbrook Park?' The Brookers' family estate was a large and beautiful one.

'No. At Kingston Manor.'

'The house your grandmother left you?'

'We are all second sons and to tread on the toes of the heir is inevitably going to invite trouble. I want a new start, a family and a reason for living. Your propensity for wise investment has left us all rich, Oliver, and for that I am entirely grateful as it gives us other options.'

Oliver thought of his own brother and their troubles and he also thought of the work he was doing in Whitechapel. A new path. A different way. Even Freddie was nodding in agreement.

'The years of wild excess were much more alluring when we were younger. Now there is a sort of dullness in it all. On my part I am wondering if a visit to the Americas might pull things into place. I spoke with Alberton the other night—he could not say enough about the adventures he had had and it sounded like a country full of opportunity.'

Sarah Barrington-Hall and one of her friends, Miss Hannah Alton, had joined their small group now and close up Oliver saw that Esther's cousin held the same sort of classical beauty as the rest of her family. Her smile was warm as she moved in beside Barrett.

'When did you arrive, Mr Brooker?' Her voice held a similar cadence to Esther's.

'Ten minutes ago. Would you like to dance?'

'Indeed I would.'

When the girl next to her looked uncertain Barrett leapt in. 'Oliver, could you partner Miss Alton?'

'I would be delighted to.' He held out his hand, a gesture gratefully responded to and the next moment he was on the dance floor, the music of the waltz all around him.

Esther Barrington-Hall glided by in the arms of Lord Alberton, as did her cousin Benjamin, with a woman he had no recognition of.

Noticing his gaze, Miss Alton was quick to comment. 'We are surrounded by the Barrington-Halls, Mr Moreland, and quite a force they are, too. Miss Esther, in particular, is extraordinarily lovely and she, Sarah and Charlotte are very close.'

'So it seems.' He did not want to talk about Esther with her, but the girl went on.

'My brother says that Lord Alberton is very taken by her. Sarah insists, however, that her cousin will not be rushing into any formal union straight away.'

Now this was more interesting. 'You are saying she will be testing the waters, so to speak?'

Nervous laughter followed. 'If I were as beautiful as Esther Barrington-Hall, I certainly would be.'

He smiled. Hannah Alton was pretty enough in her own right, but every woman in the room seemed to pale into oblivion beside Esther. She was nothing like she had appeared all those years before when he had met her with her mother, dark circles beneath her eyes and fear within them. A small, thin girl who held herself as still as she was able to.

As the dance finished he escorted Miss Alton back to her friends and thanked her, pleased to escape the dance floor and glad also to see Freddie only a few feet away. Esther was nowhere in sight.

Oliver Moreland stood over to one side of the room with Mr Bronson. She'd seen him dancing with Sarah's friend Hannah Alton, and they looked as though they had much to say to one another.

He was drinking quite steadily, she noticed that, too, the glass he held in his hand now his second in about as many minutes. Was he a man who enjoyed alcohol with as much fervour as her mother's lovers had? The stories of him suggested this as a truth and yet she saw, too, how he favoured his left side.

Did he still smart from the accident in Hyde Park and, if so, why on earth was he here, in the crush and the hectic activity of a crowded society ball? She wished she could simply forget him, but there was the invisible tie from the past that held them together and a fascination that she was finding more and more difficult to fight.

Mr Andrew Wilfred, a friend of Benjamin's, had now come across to claim her for the next dance so she accompanied him to join in a quadrille that was about to begin. Of all the dances this was her least favourite, the constant changing of partners demanding a smile that did not waver. It took them a while to find a set that did not hold all eight members within it already and as she took her place she was horrified to see Mr Moreland standing with his aunt on the other side of the square. The very thought of dancing in such close public proximity made Esther uneasy, but she could not show it. No, she must be gracious, polite and distant. Thank God she had gloves on, was all she could think as the first notes started for the five parts to the quadrille, a dance that suddenly seemed awfully long and inescapable.

The music began with its rousing tune and the head couple walked in to meet at the centre in the first movement of Le Pantalon.

She and Andrew Wilfred were one of the side pairings still resting, as were Oliver Moreland and his aunt standing opposite.

The older woman looked over at her and smiled, but her nephew did not. Rather, he made a point of observing those dancing but did not appear at all pleased when it was their turn to come together.

Esther rounded her arms and held the sides of her skirt as she stepped forward, willing away nerves. Oliver Moreland was stiff as he joined her, a sterner expression on his face than had been there a moment before. When he took her hands in his and they twirled around she tried her best to appear nonchalant, but having him so close to her was disconcerting, the darker chips of colour in his blue eyes most noticeable. She could understand why he had so many admirers in society, for in truth she had never seen a more beautiful man, and up close and in this light he simply took her breath away.

'Are you enjoying the evening, Miss Barrington-Hall?' His tone was vaguely arrogant.

'I am, thank you, Mr Moreland.'

Formal words, sentiments that meant nothing really, but her hands burned from where he touched her, a stab of delight shooting up her arm and into her chest.

He nodded as the music broke them up again, another, older man stepping towards her. Plastering the expected smile in place, she gave her greeting, but Oliver Moreland's presence made her clumsy and she tripped up on a step.

'Sorry,' she muttered, counting her way into the next movement, by which time she had been claimed by yet another partner.

A few moments later they faced each other again.

'Did you receive my flowers?'

This question came from nowhere and she blushed. So they *were* his.

'I did, sir, and they were lovely.'

'I am sure you were sent many others, too.'

'I was, but your ones were the most interesting.'

She blurted this out and then wished that she had not. An improper confession. An unwise truth.

'Your dress was white and your eyes are green. The choice thus seemed appropriate.'

'Charlotte said exactly that. She imagined the anonymous sender to be a man who was not conventional.'

He smiled, but did not comment on her assessment of his character at all.

'My family enjoys debate and mystery and your unusual bouquet with its cryptic note provided them with much to say.'

For the first time she heard him laugh. 'They like dissention, then, and argument?'

'Secrets intrigue them, though I myself prefer agreement.'

'Because it is safer?'

She stiffened because for just a moment she felt he might have remembered her, but when he smiled she knew he had not.

'Safer than falling off a horse in Hyde Park, at least.'

'A stupid accident, I admit, though in my defence the weather was more than bad.'

'I have heard that you enjoy riding?'

'Not as much as Alberton does but no doubt he has told you of his prowess.'

'Many times,' she answered and liked it when he laughed.

They turned then into the next move and Mr Wilfred was again before her, holding out his hand to claim her attention. His grip was tight and she wished he might loosen it, but he didn't, moving even closer instead.

'You look happy, Miss Barrington-Hall.'

'Indeed, for it is a lovely ball.'

'Can I also say how much you suit the colour blue?'

'Thank you.' She did not want to hear any more compliments from him.

'Moreland does not look too worse for wear, either, which is surprising.'

'Surprising?' She did not know what else to say.

'There are whispers he was shot at in the park.'

Horror consumed her. 'By whom?'

'An enemy, I should guess, and God knows a man like him must have many.'

The music had changed now and the square re-formed in a different way, leaving her with the next man and then the next.

Finally Oliver Moreland was there beside her again, though as he turned to face back to her she could see pain in the movement.

The other women had their fans out now and she unsheathed her own, standing with him while the head couple took to the middle of the square.

'I knew a woman who broke her leg once and did not leave enough time to let it properly heal. She limped quite badly in the last months of her life because of it and barely slept.'

She said this quietly, not admitting that it was of her mother she spoke because the connection between past and present was fragile.

'Is that a salient warning, Miss Barrington-Hall?'

Was he telling her to mind her own business? Oliver Moreland was not a man whom she understood, not a soft man, either, who would take advice and modify his behaviour.

He was struggling, but wanted no one else to know.

That truth hit her distinctly.

'I am saying that I do not believe you are quite as recovered from your recent accident as you may think, and that a dance as long and complicated as the quadrille is not perhaps the best exercise to be participating in.'

His shock made her smile, but the music changed and she shifted to the next partner, pretending enjoyment and all the while observing Oliver Moreland becoming more and more pale, the bruising around his right eye appearing darker because of it.

Something had to be done!

She waited till he was beside her again, and then, turning her right foot inwards, she simply fell down to the ground, landing in a lather of blue floating silk, her fan slapping to the floor.

He leant down immediately, his hand out helping her up, a look in his eyes that she could not interpret at all.

'Could you please find me a seat, Mr Moreland? I appear to have injured my ankle.' She made sure her voice was heard by the pair next to her as she dusted chalk from her shoe.

'Of course.' He led her away and set back a chair from an empty table, helping her into it.

The others continued with the dance, though Esther made a point of not meeting the eyes of Mr Wilfred, who was now paired with Julia Buckley, the older woman keeping him to the steps with a stream of chatter. She was pleased that a couple from those watching had joined the group to make up the required number so that the dance could at least continue.

Sitting, Esther saw Oliver Moreland frown.

'I feel you may have fallen on purpose, Miss Barrington-Hall?' There was both question and puzzlement in his words and she tipped up her face to his.

'Well, the fifth movement is more taxing than all the rest put together, and I doubt you would have made it through to the end. When you gave the impression you needed some much-sought-after respite, I decided to provide it.'

He stilled. 'Like a guardian angel?'

His words were direct and candid, no artifice in them at all, but her aunt, now ten yards away, was coming towards them, her face a picture of concern. Everywhere people were looking, waiting for what might happen next, surprised probably that the jaded and cynical Oliver Moreland had taken the time and care to provide an unpractised debutante with a much-needed seat.

And then he was gone.

Aunt Mary was beside her, her expression guarded.

'Are you hurt badly, Esther? I saw you take a tumble.'

'My foot felt momentarily strange and could not

bear my weight. An old injury that is sometimes troubling.'

'You are wise to rest, then, my dear, though I did wonder why it was Mr Moreland and not your partner, Mr Wilfred, who helped you from the floor.'

Her aunt looked around in order to see who was near. 'A man like Oliver Moreland is not to be played with, Esther. He could make you a dangerous enemy.'

Such a change in tone astounded her.

'Enemy?'

'Your father married a woman whom he should not have and look what happened there.'

Esther's heartbeat quickened. This was the first she had ever heard her aunt speak of her mother in such terms and it was not flattering.

'I barely know him.'

'Then make sure it stays like that.' Her aunt's face held censure and the night seemed to fold in on itself, crinkling like paper, all sharp edges with no sense in it.

Aunt Mary was warning her off Mr Moreland? Had she seen something Esther thought well hidden, some expression on her face that might not have been guarded enough? Details were always the things that tripped you up in the end.

Alexandra's reticule open on a table, a loaded pistol within plain and awful sight. The beginning of the end and the start of all that was to happen next.

Shaking her head, Esther came back to the present. Lord Alberton was here now, all solicitous alarm as he enquired after her health. Across the room she could see Mr Moreland, but dragged her eyes away, given the proximity of her aunt, and turned.

'My ankle feels much better now,' she made herself say, and took the hand of Lord Alberton as she stood. 'I should have danced the quadrille with you, my lord, for I may not have fallen then.' Deflections came in many forms and as the child of a woman who had little idea of consequences Esther had honed the art to perfection.

Already Aunt Mary looked happier and Lord Alberton happier again.

The night's jagged pieces began to reform themselves, a smoother contentment overriding the disturbing and alarming dance with Oliver Moreland.

With him she said things that were not hidden, voicing wild thoughts that could only lead to trouble, and when he had helped her up from the floor it was as if a shutter had dropped and she'd seen right into his soul, an uncertainty in his dark blue eyes that was astonishing.

The quadrille had finally finished and Mr Wilfred was departing in the other direction, Julia Buckley on her own pathway to her nephew's side. No one looked pleased.

Esther knew Mr Moreland's aunt had kept Mr Wilfred as her partner even though he had made an attempt to come over and help her. Why had the woman done that?

The undercurrent of things not being quite right kept mounting and Aunt Mary's warning was one not to be ignored. Signs were something Esther held great faith in after her upbringing for she had lived by premonitions just as surely as Alexandra had died by disregarding them.

Instinct had been the one guiding light that had brought her back to safety, to Aunt Mary and Uncle Thomas, away from chaos, danger and poverty, and she would never discount the feeling.

The whole night had been troubling, so she squared her shoulders and tightened her fingers on the sleeve of Lord Alberton, glad of his presence beside her.

She wished the evening would soon be over so that she could return to St James's Square, away from all the complications of society. A swell of noise alerted her to some other happening in the room even as Lord Alberton spoke.

'God,' he whispered. 'This is all the night needs. The Earl of Elmsworth is here with his wife.'

'Elmsworth?'

'Moreland's older brother. They generally seldom grace the same event and I cannot imagine the Keegans had the audacity to invite them both knowing how they feel about each other, so Phillip must have come on his own accord.'

The tall, dark man who had walked into the room was almost as handsome as his brother and the woman on his arm was the loveliest Esther had ever laid her eyes on.

'Her name is Gretel, Lady Elmsworth,' Alberton said as he saw her interest. 'She conquered her Season eight years ago as an Original and the Earl snapped her up as his wife in the first week of meeting her. As yet, though, they have had no children to ensure the succession of an heir.'

Where was Oliver Moreland, was Esther's next thought, and she looked around trying to see in which part of the large room he was.

When she found him she knew he had seen his brother for he was faced away from the couple and in the company of the same man he had been with earlier, and he was standing very still.

He was with a friend, at least. Surely that would stop him from doing anything too foolish?

The Earl was largely alone with his wife. A few people had wandered over to him, but the great majority of them stood back, watching and wondering just how this was going to play out.

But then Gretel Elmsworth pulled away from her husband and made her way to her brother-in-law's side, her thin face full of hope.

It was like watching a play performed in public, the tragedy, the anguish and the anticipation, Oliver Moreland standing stiffly in the very middle of it looking neither comfortable nor thrilled to see her. He was trying his best to avoid an awkward scene, Esther thought, because so very often she had been in the same sort of situation with her mother and she had acted in the very same way.

Without thought Esther stepped forward, but then stopped. It would not help him or her to be the centre of another scandal and there was nothing at all she could do now to aid the perplexing Oliver Moreland.

*   *   *

He knew his brother was in the room almost instantly, the old knowledge of each other coming to the fore, and if his first thought was to leave, his second was that of standing his ground. London was his home just as Elmsworth Manor on the Hampshire lands was Phillip's.

'Your brother is here,' Freddie said in a quiet voice.

'I know.'

'His wife is coming over.'

Oliver felt anger rise and then she was there beside him, thinner than he remembered her, but every bit as beautiful.

'Please could we talk, Oliver?'

'Last time we talked I got a bullet for my trouble, so I imagine we have all said as much as we need to, Lady Elmsworth.'

He used her name unkindly. He could hear the sneer of it in his own words.

'The shooting was a terrible mistake and Phillip has suffered for it every day since. When we heard you had an accident yesterday in Hyde Park, he insisted on coming to town...'

'To finish the job?'

'To beg your forgiveness before it is too late.'

This was getting out of hand, Oliver thought, and hoped like hell they might both just leave. A crowded public room wasn't the time to air the dirty Moreland family laundry.

'A society ball is not the place to thrash out our family differences.'

'Well, you won't come to us, so…'

'I think you know one of the reasons why, Gretel.'

She coloured, distinctly, and her glance dropped away from his own.

Then she was gone, walking across to his brother and taking his arm. Phillip did not look over at all and a moment later they left, the room relaxing back into a more normal chatter, the music restarting.

Why the hell had he been so unpleasant? He knew the answer as soon as he asked the question. He wanted them gone because he could not bear the thought of Esther Barrington-Hall understanding the truth of his fractured family, the sordidness and the disrepute.

All around him he could hear the whispers, gossip having a certain cadence of secrecy. All the old stories would surface again no doubt, his father's anger, his mother's madness. Phillip and he had been caught between their emotion for years, two brothers trying to make sense of parents who had all but destroyed them.

Lady Duggan caught his eye as he turned, the frown across her forehead deep. He knew that Mary Duggan had seen the exchange between her niece and himself during the steps of the quadrille and she was unsettled. Esther probably knew of her feelings, too, because their body language after he had left them spoke of warnings and caution.

He could not approach Esther again, as much as he would like to. He needed to leave her completely alone with the suitable young men who had swarmed around her, Lord Alberton the leader of the pack.

Her face was turned up to him now, in welcome, and she had not left his side. A safe harbour, he supposed, and after the upbringing she had likely had, then who could blame her?

Not him, at least.

'The Barrington-Hall girl keeps reeling you in, Oliver, and you are like a fish who refuses to let go of the line.'

Frederick was back beside him, and try as he might, he could not find his more usual detachment.

'Esther Barrington-Hall fell in the quadrille to relieve me of the necessity of the dance.'

'She told you that?'

'She did.'

'I am presuming that there are things you are not telling me. About her.'

'How long have we known each other for, Frederick?'

'Well, we are both twenty-five, so fifteen years and counting.'

'A long time.'

'Long enough for trust, at least, Oliver.'

As a servant walked by with a tray laden with drinks, he took two of the tall glasses and handed one to Freddie.

'To friendship, then.' He lifted his glass and drank, and the night looked like an easier one than it had been a few moments before.

Chapter Four

The carriage ride home to St James's Square was awkward, her aunt's silence complete and the rest of the family tiptoeing around her displeasure.

'Do you have a headache, Mary, my dear?' Her uncle's words held concern.

'No. It has just been a disappointing night.'

Esther knew this was in reference to her, and she looked out of the window.

'Well, the Elmsworth brothers livened it up for you, surely.' Sarah's voice held laughter. 'Though it would have been even better had they come to fisticuffs. I think on reflection, though, the victory could be chalked up to Oliver Moreland for standing his ground and dispatching the Earl and his wife off fairly promptly.'

'Just another example of their poor morals and manners.' Aunt Mary finally spoke and once she started she could not stop. 'I pity anyone who becomes entangled in their constant battles. It is plainly obvious that they are not a family to be encouraged at all.'

More words for her ears alone, Esther thought.

'Your brother and his wife had the very same problems, Thomas. They did not believe in the rules of society and look where that got them.'

Sarah and Charlotte rolled their eyes at each other, but Esther was mortified. She did not want to feel like this tonight, the music of the ball still in her ears and a childhood that had been abysmal encroaching.

She did not wish for Aunt Mary and Uncle Thomas to fight, either, because she knew underneath that she was the very reason that they were. A lump rose in her throat and she swallowed, trying to push the past back, trying to regain a lightness.

Charlotte's hand came into hers and Esther breathed out. She could see Aunt Mary watching, a line of worry on her brow and her mouth tight. She remembered her mother doing the very same thing even as she reached for another drug or a half-empty bottle that would transport her back into the oblivion she craved.

It had been a dark night very like this one when Oliver Moreland had found them huddled in the little doorway off Pall Mall, the snow falling, the temperatures plummeting. The man had hit her mother hard three times across her face as he had left her bed, her bare limbs splayed out pale in the semi-darkness. He had called Mama names, too, words Esther had no understanding of, but the tone had been harsh and bitter, his fury frightening.

She had got her mother dressed and pulled her from the house, before the man returned, before he could apologise, before Mama could mutter more of her excuses and promises.

And when Oliver Moreland had taken them from a doorway on those dangerous streets and whisked them back to the room they rented in Camden Town, all Esther had felt was relief.

Her saviour. A second chance.

She had no way of knowing then, of course, that the promises of a future that came so readily to Alexandra's lips would never be kept and that the man with the heavy fists would return, again and again.

'We are home, Esther.' Sarah's words brought her back, the door of the carriage opening and the steps pulled into place.

Home. For the first time since she had arrived at the town house of her uncle and aunt's in St James's Square, Esther was not sure if it would be hers for very much longer.

The flowers were there in her room, the green sage and the white roses, fuller now than they had been the day before, yellow stamens on show and their perfume more pronounced.

She trailed her fingers across the velvety petals, feeling their fragility. With care she then brought the bouquet up to breathe in deeply. A number of the petals dropped to the floor by her feet, more cream than white now and wilted.

'Help me,' she whispered. 'Help me to be braver.'

The clock chimed two and her candle flickered. A breeze, she supposed, from the window for she could hear the wind rising. She should undress and get into bed, but a maid had not yet arrived and she was glad of it for she wanted to sit here and think, of Oliver Moreland's hands against hers, of his smile and his scent. She wanted to understand him and know him because although her aunt was certain he was dissolute and degenerate, she was just as sure that he was not.

He had saved her on the street that night, rescued them from hell, and she would never ever forget that he had. She would speak of it next time she saw him, she promised herself that she would, and thank him again from the bottom of her heart. If such a truth broke open chaos, then she would be prepared for that, too. One could not live in a lie without being damaged and she saw suddenly that all the veneers her aunt had tried to erect in order to protect her were thin things, woven only in luck.

A suitor like Alberton would not want to know her truths and so she would be forced to stay in deceit for ever should she throw her hand in with him or with any of the other young men here in society who had asked her for a dance.

Oliver Moreland would not betray her.

She stood at that thought. It was in his eyes as he thanked her, this certainty. He would protect her just as she had protected him.

A truce.

The night felt easier and when the maid came to ready her for bed she turned and smiled.

Oliver spent the night tossing and turning alone in bed. His side ached and the gash that the fence in Hyde Park had left on his leg when he had hit it throbbed. His head thumped, too, and his right eye felt bruised and hot.

He should not have attended the Keegans' ball and his aunt had castigated him before he had left it. Julia. He knew she meant the best for him, but sometimes he could hear his mother's voice in her words: disappointment and frustration.

The dance kept coming back into his mind, Esther Barrington-Hall in his arms and the softness of holding her. Blue should not have suited her with the colour of her green eyes, but it did. It showed off all the hues in her hair and the clear, fine perfectness of her skin.

When she had fallen he'd wanted to simply sweep her up and take her with him from the room, away from everyone, somewhere far and safe and alone.

The thought of the ring she had given him came back and, finding his clothes and roughly dressing, he left the bedchamber to look for the lost trinket. He found it in the third drawer of the desk in his library, stored with other baubles he had long outgrown, but did not quite wish to give away.

It was smaller than he remembered, the gold thinner and more tarnished than it had been in recall. The young Esther had held it in the palm of her hand in uncertainty and then left it among the wool of the carriage blanket. In payment.

Turning the ring to the light he read the inscription.

M.P. 1796

Her father's initials, perhaps, for it was too big a size for a woman. Had Esther received this after his death and taken it when her mother had left the family estate with her in tow? She was nineteen now, he had heard someone say at the Creighton ball. So 1796 might have been the year of her father's marriage.

He had never heard a whisper of anything untoward about the Barrington-Halls. No, they were a family steeped in tradition, good manners and strong morals. Julia had said the younger brother of Thomas had liked his wine overmuch, but then so did half of those in society.

And yet…the woman he had helped transport from London to Camden Town six years before had hardly looked respectable with her blackened eye and split lip. Her gown had been stained, too, down one whole side, a dark blemish that spoke of harder times and difficult circumstances. She had smelt of sweat and dankness.

Could he ask Esther about her mother, for there was no doubt she had recognised him at the Creightons' ball? Or would she deny such a connection, the truth of what lay behind it too destructive?

She had tried to help him on the dance floor with her unexpected fall, but she had also looked horrified to see her aunt hurrying towards them with anger on her face.

When one terrible storm was survived, there was not often the want to ride into another. He understood that himself because of the relationships inside his own family. Sometimes there was just no going back to try to smooth the waters, and when the waves broke across you, all you could do was take one gulp of air at a time and hope like hell that the tempest would not last for ever and you could surface again to live.

Was that how Esther Barrington-Hall had felt in the carriage that night all those years ago as she had helped her mother in and then offered up the ring in payment?

His fingers curled around the thin gold. Had she been hurt, too, the man who had smashed his fist into her mother's face presumably a dangerous and unstable character?

He swore as he stalked back to his chamber. There would be no rest for him tonight with all these old memories swirling around, so he might as well go to the place where at least he was welcome.

When he gained his room he took the knife in the drawer by his bed and fastened the straps just in the way he liked them around his ankle. Taking his heavy coat from the wardrobe he buttoned it up, grabbed his hat and was gone.

An hour later he sat with Michael Tomlinson in his office looking at the ledgers of the St Mary's Children's Home, a warm fire in the grate to one side of the room.

'You and I have made a big difference, Oliver, in the lives of these children. I hope you know that?'

Oliver smiled and nodded. 'And I will continue to do so.'

'But we have also made enemies of those who profit from the horrors of the workhouses. Billy Finnegan, in particular, is spouting vitriol about our work here and he is a dangerous man who has other, more stupid men that follow him. The other week in the park when we were riding and the shot came from nowhere...' He tailed off.

'You think it could have been him?'

He saw Tomlinson's eyes glance at the bulge at his left ankle.

'A knife might not be enough any more. There are others, too, in Finnegan's employ who want us both gone from these streets, violent and aggressive men.'

'I think you are in more danger here, Michael, for this is where you live and work. I will be fine.'

'But people talk and they are talking more than they used to. We have accrued a following of grateful recipients from the money you are meting out and therein lies the problem. The old ways are being threatened and people like Billy Finnegan think that a betterment of this place will lead to their own demise and that the power of violence will fail.'

'Just as they think every child who benefits from an education threatens them more?'

'It's an unfair world, Oliver. We can't change everything and all at once.'

He laughed. 'Unfair both here and in the salons of society, Michael, but then you would know about that.'

'It's a long time since I left my old life and I'll never go back.' Michael looked at him with his steady gaze.

'I'm starting to feel the same.'

'When I was younger this is exactly what I wanted

to do, and without your help I could not have. Remember at Eton we used to talk about our dreams all the time, Oliver? I thought yours were of working the land?'

'God, that was a while ago. Phillip has Elmsworth Manor now.'

'I heard.'

'He tried to shoot me last year.'

'In your side, wasn't it? In and out without touching an organ. How is it now?'

'You knew?'

'The doctor that Freddie found, the one who attended you, was a friend of mine.'

'Thank God, then, for the ethics inherent in the Hippocratic oath. Otherwise the news may have been all over London.'

'You don't hate Phillip, then?'

'He's my brother, Michael.'

'You were always my most complex friend. Let's have a brandy before we go through these figures again. It will probably help.'

Oliver looked at the clock. 'It's late.'

'That's fine, because I seldom sleep well.'

'You never did much, if I recall.'

'A state which is a bonus when one has sick patients to tend to.'

'Or friends who come calling at hours they should not?'

'You are welcome here at any time of the day or night, my friend.'

'Thank you.'

* * *

'By God, but doesn't Oliver Moreland travel around in all the strange hours?'

Esther heard her cousin Jeremy say this as she walked past his bedroom door and knew he was speaking with Ben. Despite her intention not to, she stood still and listened.

'Did you see him, then?'

'I did last night from the window of my carriage at one in the morning on his steed turning into the streets of Whitechapel. What would he be doing in that neck of the woods, for heaven's sake? The place is a hellhole and barely fit for animals.'

Benjamin's voice was dubious. 'I doubt that one of his unsuitable ladybirds would be living in that quarter. There are murders there aplenty in the daylight, so goodness knows what it is like to venture into after dark.'

'A den of iniquity, I would guess, which seems a suitable hangout for Moreland. Perhaps he makes his fortune off the misery of others, in opium or strong spirits?'

Ben began to laugh. 'You have been reading too many broadsheets, Brother, for his money comes in from a steady stream of the wise investments he is known to have made. Maybe, in truth, he is simply unable to sleep?'

'Well, he certainly seemed interested in Esther at the ball last night, Ben, but then so did every other man present. Perhaps I am reading too much into it.'

'Or not. I know that Mama wasn't happy when

our cousin fell in the quadrille and into his arms, for I think she has high hopes of Alberton offering for her hand.'

'Chances are he will and Esther will be doomed for ever to speak of horseflesh and stables for the rest of her life.'

'Perhaps he should marry Charlotte, then, for I am sure she would be delighted to have a constant conversation on such things.'

'No, I think even our youngest sister might become bored with his long monologues. He has got worse since his return from the Americas, don't you think?'

Esther moved as the laughter came closer, not wanting to be caught out eavesdropping, yet unsettled by everything they had said.

Whitechapel was known for its crime and for its squalor, a place so degenerate that even her mother had known to stay away from it. What could Mr Moreland have possibly gone there for? The very idea that he might be involved in illicit dealings made her feel sick and she reached out to steady herself. There was so much that she did not know about him.

Her aunt nearly bumped right into her as she rounded the corner, though this morning she looked back to her normal happy self.

'I thought we might go with Charlotte and Sarah to Gunter's tea shop this morning, my love. I think we need to get out with just the four of us and away from the men for at least an hour or two. What do you say?'

'I would like that.'

'Then go and get ready and see if the girls want to

come, too. I am certain that they will because I heard them complaining earlier of being stuck at home on such a grey day.'

An hour later the four of them were at a table in Gunter's tea shop in Berkeley Square, a plate of pastries in the middle of the table.

'It is not a day for ices and sorbets, girls, but one for the delicious concoctions of almond marzipan and hazelnut chocolate. My idea is that if we finish this plate we will simply order another and then another after that if we so wish it.' Aunt Mary said this as she finished off her second almond marzipan. 'Today we shall not worry at all about gluttony, greediness or our figures. We shall only enjoy.'

All around them were people, the tables full to brimming as if every other fashionable family had been thinking the exact same thing as they had, needing a break from the vagaries of the winter weather.

Esther was glad she did not recognise most of them, though the Hamilton girls sat in one corner and another woman she knew by sight rather than by name in another.

'Lady Beaumont sent me a letter yesterday saying that she has asked others up to the house party as well. It seems from what she says that there will be quite a number of people and I should imagine the party to include an array of young people of good breeding.'

Sarah knew exactly where her mother was leading. 'If it's matchmaking you are alluding to, Mama, I want you to know that I shan't be participating at all.'

Aunt Mary frowned. 'And pray tell me why is that, my dear?'

'Because I think I might have finally found a man who does not bore me and one who makes my heart beat faster.'

Charlotte almost squealed with delight, earning a rebuke from her mother.

'And are we allowed to know this man's name?'

'Of course.' Sarah smiled. 'It is Mr Brooker. I have known him for a month or so, but recently we have become closer.'

'Of the wealthy Brookers to the north of London?' Aunt Mary was quick to make the connection. 'Well, that may indeed be fortuitous for I am sure the family is related to the Beaumonts and Mr Brooker could well be receiving his own invitation, too, so we may see them all there.'

Esther could see Charlotte mulling over the name in that particular way she had of putting people into a place in society.

'Is he not a friend of Mr Moreland's, Sarah?' Charlotte asked.

'Indeed he is.'

'Then perhaps Oliver Moreland may also be invited to the Beaumonts' party. Oh, I do hope that he is, for interesting things always seem to happen around him and life never seems as dull.'

Esther could feel her aunt watching her and she sat very still. She did not wish for a repeat of the conversation from yesterday, but an excitement at the prospect of him being at the same house party began to build. She might be able to speak with him again, even if briefly.

'Well, I have no idea as to whom the Beaumonts have invited, though my own opinion is if they want an event of a certain standard they might be wise to omit Mr Moreland.' Her aunt's tone was flat.

'I think you do him a disservice, Mama,' Sarah said, 'for look how he helped Esther when she fell in the quadrille. He could not have been more of a gentleman.'

Her aunt gave no further comment, but Esther could see a 'gentleman' was the last thing she felt Oliver Moreland was. The coffee had come now and the conversation turned to the presentation of the food. Charlotte spoke at length of all the delicious cakes she had seen at different venues and Esther began to relax.

Another three weeks till the house party at the Beaumonts. Oliver Moreland would presumably be far more in health by then and an opportunity might come to have a moment alone.

Without Alberton. Her heart sank a little because in his domain Lord Alberton might expect things that she had no intention of giving. His mother, Lady Beaumont, was quite a busybody, however, and undoubtedly had her own hopes to marry off her son to a girl with a large dowry, something which she did not have.

An idea began to form as she looked over at Charlotte. Her cousin had both and she also had a huge interest in anything equestrian. With a bit of time and luck, perhaps Alberton might recognise exactly that and tip his hat at her instead.

Aunt Mary would be pleased, no doubt, and so would Lady Beaumont, both of which would leave her free to pursue her own dreams.

Picking up a miniature hazelnut chocolate, Esther slipped it into her mouth, feeling happier by the moment.

The invitation to the Beaumont house party had arrived at his town house half an hour ago. Barrett had mentioned the possibility yesterday, but it was his inclusion of the Duggan name that had really got him listening. Barrett was back again this morning and, on seeing the card, Oliver could tell his friend was most hopeful he would accompany him.

'All of the Barrington-Halls are going, and en masse the family is a lot of fun.'

'Especially Sarah Barrington-Hall?' Oliver could not help but ask that question.

But Barrett was not drawn into reply as he finished one brandy and poured himself another. 'At twenty-five, do you not have an inkling that it's time to settle down?'

Oliver thought of his conversation last evening with Michael Tomlinson and smiled as Barrett carried on.

'Bring up the drawbridge? Find the boundaries of family?'

'You are saying that you are?'

'I don't know.' For the first time he could ever remember, Barrett looked uncertain.

'I don't want to be one of those men who do not stop playing the field, those lonely men without family around them whom everyone feels sorry for eventually.'

Like his father and like Phillip. No true sense of place. Like him, too, Oliver supposed, the succession of lovers he'd had mostly empty and meaningless relationships.

'You have made a fortune in property and investments, Oliver. Would you not want to leave London and see if you could establish yourself in some quiet and green corner of England? Take up farming or local politics, perhaps, and leave the sordid side of this city far behind you?'

'It seems as if you have considered the idea in depth.'

'I have. My accounts may not be quite as prosperous as yours, but I do have my grandmother's estate.' Barrett looked serious. 'I want to get away from all the tangles that hold me here. I want freedom and my father is more than keen to have heirs to the title.'

'What of your brother?'

'He has two girls and my sister-in-law was very sick after the last birth. The place is entailed and they do not want to risk having more, so…' He stopped and took in breath. 'So the Darrington Halls will be at the Beaumont house party up in Barnet and I want to be there, too, but I was hoping you would come to give me some support as well.'

'I'd probably be a hindrance instead.'

'How?'

'Lady Duggan does not want me anywhere near her niece, so if Sarah and Esther are together…' He stopped, the whole conversation suddenly ridiculous and taking a direction he had no wont to pursue.

Barrett only laughed. 'Nothing has ever stopped you taking what you want before. Besides, the Barrington-Hall girls have a certain strength that is highly unlikely to be tempered by the likes or dislikes of Mary Duggan.'

'I'll come if I can.'

'You mean you will come if you want.'

Oliver leant forward and took out a document from a pile, unravelling it on his desk.

'I've made a new will and I need your signature on the thing tomorrow at eleven as a witness in front of my lawyer.'

'Hell. Do you think you are in some sort of danger?'

He frowned. 'I just want things tied up properly. Things are always a mess if they are not.'

'What's in it?'

'Bequests to various people, yourself included. Money for the St Mary's Home in Whitechapel and investment papers for Michael Tomlinson. A few baubles to be returned to their owners.'

Barrett walked across and looked it over and Oliver knew the moment he had reached the paragraph about Esther.

'Why are you leaving a sizeable lump sum of money to Miss Esther Barrington-Hall?'

'I want her to be safe.'

'And she isn't?'

'I'm not sure.'

'But you are not going to tell me any more?'

'No.'

'And you are giving your brother a great deal of your fortune. That's a generous settlement after all that has happened between you?'

He rolled the document up. 'You'll be here tomorrow at eleven, then, Barrett?'

'I will. And you will make the effort to be at the Beaumonts' house party for at least a few of the days?'

Oliver could hardly say no.

Chapter Five

Esther thought that the Beaumont estate was one of the most beautiful she had ever seen.

The house sat on a rising hill before a small river, the rolling lawns and rows of trees setting off the pale stone building behind them magnificently.

Every care had been taken to make sure each guest had every comfort, the beds warmed, the flowers fresh, the many servants skilled, perceptive and largely inconspicuous.

She and Charlotte were sharing a room while Sarah as the oldest daughter was in the smaller adjoining chamber, the rest of the family fanned out in different rooms on the same floor. With about thirty other guests Esther was amazed at the amount of space the house had available, for nothing seemed squashed or difficult. No, it all flowed beautifully and easily, delicious and appetising meals appearing exactly at the times stated and the entertainment well set out.

Lord Alberton had been attentive and well mannered, every conversation between them leading to more facts about the family and the estate.

Today she sat with him on the swinging chair outside the library and overlooking the western aspect of the property. When a small but chilly wind rose he doffed his jacket and laid it around her shoulders, a gentle response to the cold.

'Thank you.' She had found him more approachable out of town and less wordy about his well-stocked stables, though his stories of journeys in the Americas were always long-winded and complicated.

'It's been a long time since I enjoyed a woman's company quite as much as yours, Miss Barrington-Hall,' he said as he finished telling her of a farm machine he had seen somewhere there. 'I know it's only early days, but I do want you to know that I find you most attractive.'

She refrained from an answer, all the while thinking that perhaps it had not been quite a wise idea to come out to the garden and sit with him in the thin winter sunshine. She wished her aunt and uncle might round the corner or any one of her cousins. A distraction. A way to go back to the impersonal. A method of escape.

'All this will be mine one day, of course, this land as far as the eye can see from that direction to this one.' His hand gestured at all the far horizons from east to west.

'It is a lot to comprehend,' she muttered.

'Being the heir eventually has its advantages,'

he carried on, 'for the estate will remain whole and hearty when my parents pass away.'

'They are both young—' she said, but he cut her off.

'I will expand into crop farming. There are new ways now of raising productivity. I saw an iron plough on the east coast with interchangeable parts which would cut the time of making a field ready for sowing by a good third and I want to bring such advancements here.'

'It sounds…remarkable.' She did not think that word was quite the one she sought, but he seized upon it with an eagerness.

'Remarkable. That is just what I think. The old ways are changing and the new ones are galloping in. One man I spoke to outside Boston was about to invest in a canning factory for fruit which would revolutionise the longevity of seasonal produce. My father thinks it is better to ponder and wait and see if these things succeed, but I have no such thoughts at all of doing that. One must use one's privilege and advantage in all the ways one can, do you not think?'

'I am not sure…'

But he was not listening. 'Because to not do that will allow others to come forward and take the sting out of surprise, the very sting that I need to make a fortune.'

'You are ambitious, then?' She stared at this new side of Lord Alberton.

'I am and I need people around me who have the same sort of ambition. Bold people, single-minded people, people who will strive and push. Determined people. People who won't take no for an answer.'

Unease filled her.

'These were the sort of people who are making money in America and by God they are making a lot of it, Esther. May I call you that?'

She nodded, because another more honest reply would probably have been rude.

'Wealth has a certain protection to it, a barrier of protection if you like, between those in society and those without.'

As she had been, she and Alexandra struggling on the streets of no return?

'I would suppose one advantage of great wealth is that it allows you to help people in need?'

Her question was quietly given, but he looked at her as if she had spoken another language altogether and then began to laugh.

'Benjamin said you had a sense of humour, Esther, and I like it.'

And right at that very moment Esther realised that she was in the wrong place with the wrong man, a man who coveted things that she never would, and one who saw life in black and white while she had spent so many of her formative years in the greyness.

Lord Henry Alberton was a product of an upbringing in an English society that had never faltered, never struggled, never understood that luck or the lack of it was not a God-given thing, but a matter of circumstance and choice.

When he leant over closer she arched back. *Please,*

God, do not let him try to kiss me or touch me or say things that I do not wish to hear.

'I think we understand each other, my dear, and it is such a joy to me…'

Voices from behind made them both turn, and Charlotte and Sarah were there, laughing in the windy day, framed by familiarity. Esther had never been so grateful to see them as she scrambled up.

'There is to be a recital on the piano and your mother sent us to find you, my lord, for she knew you would want to be present.'

Alberton stood, though he did not look pleased at all.

'We will finish this talk later.' He bent to whisper this so that her cousins did not hear and departed, leaving Charlotte and Sarah to gather her in.

Sarah was quick to speak. 'A rendezvous in private in the garden might lead to things that are more intimate, Esther. Is that what you would want with Lord Alberton?' Her brown eyes watched closely.

'He is a friend, that is all.'

'Then be careful, my love, or he may get an impression he is much, much more.'

'I will.' She squeezed her cousin's hand and went with them inside to listen to the music, the dread that she had felt on the swinging garden chair with Lord Alberton dissipating.

The next morning Esther escaped the house early to walk the path by the river and to be out of the way of Henry Alberton should he wish to continue that

talk he had begun yesterday. It was only day three of
a five-day visit and the hours in front of her looked
to be increasingly fraught. Oliver Moreland had not
come after all and he would not now. The disappointment of his absence was strong in her because she had
hoped with all her heart to see him again.

She brought the collar of her coat more tightly in
around her, the breeze sharp. This was a gentle amble
of much beauty, the sky cloudy but lacking rain and
the temperatures less cold than they had been even a
week before in London.

Charlotte had gone off to visit the stables with
Lord Alberton and a few of the others, but Esther had
declined the invitation. Her aunt and uncle had taken
a trip to the local village, a waterwheel at a flour
mill having caught their attention. Sarah was with a
group of her friends in the library and the boy cousins
were somewhere else. Shooting or fishing probably,
or simply sleeping off the late nights she knew that
they had kept here, for there were many unattached
young women in the party determined in their own
way to make this holiday count and Ben, Jeremy and
Aiden were more than fair game.

The path was a little steeper now and had joined
another, larger one and she was just wondering if she
should turn around when a figure on a horse appeared
a hundred yards away, a figure she knew instantly.

She froze with disbelief.

Oliver Moreland was here? Now? Right in front
of her? He had finally come?

She watched him dismount and take up the reins

of his black horse as he covered the last yards between them.

'Good afternoon, Miss Barrington-Hall. I take it that you are alone?'

He seemed taller, less knowable out here, the limp gone and his greatcoat billowing. He seemed healthier altogether, skin bronzed from the outdoors and a lightness about him that she had not seen before.

'At least for the moment I am.' Her heartbeat quickened, all her thoughts of him across the past month coalescing into this one moment's surprise.

'Good, because I have something for you.' These words were unexpected as he dug into the pocket of his jacket beneath the heavy coat. When he extracted his hand, her father's small gold ring lay in his proffered palm.

'You knew me, then? You remembered?' She could not pretend confusion. Not with him. 'How?'

'By your eyes,' he replied softly. 'And by the way you tilt your head.'

She was doing that now and stopped instantly, an action that evoked a smile from him.

'I hope you also know that I would never hurt you.'

'I do, sir.' And she did, with all of her heart.

Lifting her hand, he pressed the ring into it before letting go and stepping back. 'This is yours, for I told you once six years ago that I did not require payment for the help given.'

Not knowing what to say, she stayed silent, thoughts whirling in her head.

'Everyone holds the sort of secrets that are easier

to simply leave behind, Miss Barrington-Hall, and I am a great believer that they should be allowed to do that.'

Such formality was just what she needed as she clutched the ring tightly in her hand. A piece of her past that could be reclaimed and without jeopardy. The unexpected lack of consequence allowed explanation.

'It was my father's. Marcus Paul. That was his name. He was my uncle's younger brother and he died when I was five.'

Oliver Moreland showed no sign of surprise and she thought perhaps he had already worked out whom the initials belonged to.

'A great sadness for you and your mother.'

'So much so that we left Redworth Manor, our home in Kent, shortly afterwards.'

She suddenly wanted him to know that she was not always homeless and that the family she had lost were people who were once gentle and dignified folk. She needed him to understand the context for all that was gone and for what was left.

The silence between them then was filled with memory and for such she was endlessly glad.

'I did not think you would come at all, even though Mr Brooker insisted that you would.' She turned the subject to other things after a moment or so.

'I nearly didn't, but Barrett is a good friend of mine and had specifically asked that I attend.'

'Well, I imagine Lady Beaumont will be thrilled to see you.'

'Why?' He sounded nonplussed.

'There are a number of young women here who are strenuously seeking marriage.'

'Including you?'

The question made her blush fiercely.

'I only meant, Mr Moreland, that you are a good prospect for those who are looking.'

As he watched her Esther thought that he was so beautiful she could barely breathe. Beautiful and impossible because if she lost her heart to him he would break it. She knew that he would, break it into little pieces with no hope of any repair.

'How is it that Alberton has let you out of his sight even for a second, Miss Barrington-Hall?'

There, it was begun. A gentle reminder of his lack of true interest in the face of Alberton's pursuit. Already she could feel a tiny chink shearing off her heart as she swallowed and made herself smile, the old veils easily found.

'He is one of the hosts here so he has duties to his other guests.'

'A decided boon.'

She did not quite know how to take that remark.

'May I accompany you back to the house?'

'Of course. It is not far.'

His horse whinnied as a flock of birds rose to one side of them, startling her.

'Merlin is temperamental sometimes, but he is a good horse. Do you ride?'

'I don't.' With him she was honest. She eyed the huge stallion with trepidation.

'You don't like horses?' He began to laugh. 'My God, I imagine Alberton has been talking only of them since you arrived. It is by far his favourite subject.'

'He thinks perhaps that I used to ride.'

'Did you?'

'No. I have never even sat up on a horse.'

'And would you want to?'

'I am not sure.'

'My advice would be to begin with a gentle mare, one who is not distracted. I am sure your host must have at least one excellent candidate in his stables.'

She looked away. Alberton again. She should have kept the tone of their conversation going, the one of expediency, distance and sense, but she just could not, as the personal crept in like a thief.

'It is good to see you looking so very much better, Mr Moreland.'

He turned towards her. 'I want to thank you properly for your help in the quadrille when you saw me struggling. I shouldn't have come to the Keegans' ball that night, but...' He stopped and swallowed.

'But...?' She said the word quietly because it held such question.

'But I wanted to meet you again. I wanted to see if you remembered...'

'The carriage ride on a snowy night and your part in aiding us? How could I have forgotten that?'

'Your mother...?' He stopped himself even as he started and looked away. 'It is your business, of course, and if you do not wish to say anything of it I will understand.'

But she wanted to talk, desperately.

'Mama was sick. She enjoyed alcohol as much as my father did and she liked other things as well.'

She could not say about the inappropriate lovers or the drugs that Alexandra procured more and more often. She looked at him then, right into his dark blue eyes, and thought if he looked repulsed by the words she had given she would leave. Immediately.

But the sorrow on his face was genuine. 'I should have maybe helped you more, then. I almost came back to find you.'

'No. Mama would not have allowed it. She still had some pride left.'

'As well as a black eye and split lip?'

'That, too.'

'And you were scared?'

'The world is a frightening place for a child caught in chaos, but Camden Town allowed us a refuge, at least for a while.'

'Hell,' he swore, and she saw him swallowing, saw the muscles on the ridges of his jaw rippling. 'If you had said something—'

She stopped him by raising her hand. 'I was only twelve, and Mama believed in privacy.'

'The sort of privacy that allowed her to take you into danger and keep you there? For how long?'

'Uncle Thomas found me in London when I was thirteen.'

'And your mother?'

'Was dead.'

Catching her hand, he held it, his fingers cradling

her own. She felt both his warmth and strength and looked up.

'I would have protected you, Esther. At least believe that of me.'

'I do.'

He stepped forward and for one wild moment she thought he might take her into his arms, but of course he did not. Everything around disappeared into nothingness, the wind stilled, the sunshine faded. In the silence she could hear only the sound of a hope inside that had long been dulled, a small crack of resilience opening up that allowed it to worm through. People were coming towards them now, she could see them in the distance, her cousin Sarah and others, but she still had a moment and so she chanced it.

'I knew after meeting you at the Creightons that you would not betray me and I want to thank you for it.'

Tipping his head in acknowledgment, he let her go and they stood there waiting for the others to come closer, a silence between them that was full of meaning.

'Oliver. My God, I had completely given up on your coming.' Barrett Brooker spoke first. 'It is good to see you here and my chamber has an extra bed already made up.' Bringing Sarah forward, he smiled widely. 'You met Miss Sarah Barrington-Hall at the Keegans'.'

Esther watched Oliver Moreland's charm surface as he took her cousin's hand, an appeal that was both practised and adept. She had seen this of him in the ballrooms, the accomplished man full of fascination and magnetism. She preferred the man she had seen a moment ago, more vulnerable, less invincible. Sarah smiled at him in delight and the two women with her cousin did the same.

And in that second Esther knew that Oliver Moreland was lethal, his smile neither false nor overdone, the thin line of a seamless acknowledgement belying any hint of his reputation. Her next thought was that he knew exactly what he was doing, a sophisticated aristocrat who had played by his own rules for years and years and had got away with it.

Perhaps he was handling her in the same way, with his smooth words and unexpected flowers. She was a fleeting interest, a puzzle to be solved, a slight past guilt that needed assuaging before he could move on to greener pastures and more exciting women.

Her mother had fallen for men who played roles and look what had happened there. They had worn her down month after month, deceptive men who only thought of themselves and what they might take from her—until Alexandra had nothing left to give, save a bullet from the loaded stolen gun.

The world tilted and Esther was shocked she had allowed herself to remember that moment, here among a party of happy guests, the sound of gunfire reverberating down through the years to this beautiful and gentle estate in the English countryside.

Her fingers went to her throat and she felt the quick and rapid beat of her heart under the same old stabbing pain of shock.

* * *

Esther Barrington-Hall appeared pale and Oliver wondered why her cousin Sarah had not noticed. He couldn't step in without causing much comment, though he did toy with the idea of grabbing her hand. If she began to fall he would catch her, that much he did know.

She did not look at him, either, and the calm she was trying to convey was exactly the sort that he had always used in any difficult situation himself.

'Never allow others to know what you are thinking.' His mother's words came back unbidden. *'Keep your distance and you will be safe.'* And he always had been, this detachment a fault his many lovers complained about. He moved away as soon as they demanded more. A protection, he supposed, a way to stay secure. He did not need the worry of experiencing the deep raft of emotions that had sent his mother into the lake.

So he was glad when Barrett excused himself from the group, indicating he would accompany him to make his presence known to the host family.

Tipping his head, he walked away with his friend, resisting the urge to glance around at Esther, to see her eyes and the soft roundness of her face. Her innocence astounded him anew after such a childhood, her pureness a part of her that he could only harm. He walked away with the same sort of feeling he often knew in Whitechapel. One of being exactly where he should be despite all the difficulties.

The house before them was large and imposing,

and Merlin pulled against the reins as if he wished to gallop in freedom across the expansive green lawns that trailed up from the river.

'A grand estate,' Oliver said, for in truth there were not many others as well presented as this one.

Barrett nodded. 'I thought the same when I first saw it. I thought you should also know that Alberton has set his cap most firmly at Sarah's cousin, Esther, though there are whispers about her.'

'Whispers?'

'I have heard it said that her life has not been as easy as it looks now and Sarah herself says her cousin is trying to find a peace that has been hard-sought. She says that Alberton is a man who could bring her that with his manners and his money. She also states her mother thinks it is a very fine match and if a wife had to endure hours of speaking about every horse on earth, then it still might be worth it.'

'A warning kindly meant.'

'But meant, none the less. By the way, I found the bullet.'

The words shocked Oliver.

'It was lodged in the tree behind where you fell. From a musket, I would guess, a gun that is easy to procure and cheap.'

'Then it wouldn't have been Phillip's.'

'Someone from Whitechapel, then? Opium makes fools of some men and monsters of others. You must have enemies there with all the work you are doing trying to clean things up?'

'I do.'

'Which explains the urgency on the will you had me witness. Someone had already taken a shot at you and you thought they might try again?'

Oliver swallowed down anger because here in the sunshine on the green lawns of a fine estate he needed to think of other things, happier times, softer hopes.

But Barrett was not finished. 'Whoever it is with a gripe against you won't stop there.'

'I know, but in this moment I am safe. Would you not agree, Barrett?'

'Safe from a marksman, at least, though I am not sure about others who will be hunting you in a different way.'

'Women?'

'Exactly.'

They were at the front steps now, a large flight of stone leading up to an impressive portico.

'Well, let's go in and meet the Beaumonts. The mother has a certain desperation about her and the father will want to know the minute details of your bank account. On that score you should pass without any problems at all.'

An hour later Oliver met Esther again, this time in the hallway on the first floor after he had come down from the room he shared with Barrett.

'Your chamber is on this floor?' He looked around to see where she might have come from.

'It is.' She pointed to a portal a few yards away, a deep blush on her face. 'Just there.'

He hoped like hell that her aunt or a cousin might

not suddenly appear through it, so as to allow them a few moments alone, but the door stayed firmly shut.

'Grafton Manor is a large house and the Beaumonts seem well served by it.' It was unlike him to feel tongue-tied, but he was as he searched for a topic between them that was a safe one.

'Lord Alberton has many dreams for its future.' Dimples appeared in her cheeks as she spoke first.

'I have heard about them from many people.'

She laughed at that, the sound joyous and free. 'I rather thought that you might have.'

'Ambition is only one step, though, for without following it up with hard work it seldom comes to anything.'

'You sound learned on the subject. What ambitions do you harbour, Mr Moreland?'

'Well, they have in truth changed of late, so that question is hard to answer. Were I to be honest, I might say I now want a quieter life.'

'You will not find much peace at Grafton Manor for it is such a constant round of entertainment that silence feels like a forbidden commodity.'

The light from the window showed up in her hair, and her eyes were sparkling. Green like emeralds, translucent in their depths, rare and brilliant. He could see so clearly why so many people were fascinated by Esther Barrington-Hall's eyes, but behind them lay wit and cleverness and that fascinated him even more.

'Is Elmsworth an estate like this one?' Her next query was unexpected.

'No, it is much less...perfect.'

'Like in a fairy tale, then? A castle lost in time?'
Hesitating, she looked around and then went on. 'My
aunt and uncle's house sounds a bit like your estate.
Wonderful and complete in itself.'

'Elmsworth Manor is not mine.' He questioned
why he had said that to her, so honestly and without
any regret. Unlike Esther with her childhood home,
he had never held much of a connection to the Moreland family house and lands. 'My brother, Phillip,
inherited the property as the oldest son.'

'The man I saw at the Keegan Ball?'

'An awkward experience, no doubt, for everyone
there hoped for a volatile scene that could be digested
at leisure and at length the next morning over breakfast. In his favour Phillip seldom comes into town so
we almost never meet, but I am sure that my brother
would have wanted theatricals as little as I did.'

'Families are complicated things.'

'Yours looks fairly simple. I am sure most of society would envy the Barrington-Halls' closeness.'

'Do you, Mr Moreland?'

'Are you always so direct, Miss Barrington-Hall?'
he countered.

'Only with you,' she said then and the words fell
into the space between them with a raw and startling honesty.

His aunt's words at the Creighton ball came back
to him. *'I wonder why she felt safe to let you observe
who she really was.'*

Oliver understood the answer now. It was because
he knew her past so she did not have to pretend she

was someone else entirely different, which was a powerful freedom.

But before he had time to give an answer she was speaking again.

'But I need to tell you that I am changed now, and that frightened little girl you met on a snowy night is long gone and I am glad that she is.'

'A new Miss Esther Barrington-Hall evolving in her stead?'

She was raising her protections and he needed to let her. It is what he himself had done, after all, after his mother had died. In truth, he had probably been doing it ever since.

'A necessary transition if I wish to take my place in society. Which, I assure you, I do.'

'Once bitten, twice shy? Then the Beaumonts' social status should suit you perfectly and I wish you well.'

'Thank you.'

If there was anger in her green eyes it was only momentary, a quick flash and then gone before she turned again for her room.

He wanted to call her back, but he didn't.

She felt the tears before they fell and brushed them away with her sleeve as she entered her room. Oliver Moreland was not the man for her and never would be. He had just told her that and she needed to believe him.

He was exactly the man everyone said that he was, a man who did not commit to anything, a wanderer who allowed people close for a moment before pushing them away. She did not need a rolling stone, she needed a husband who would stay beside her through thick and thin, who would cherish her and protect her and allow her to flourish within the boundaries of polite society.

Because it was here that she meant to stay, close to her family in a place of conventions and manners and rules, a setting that did not invite chaos or ruin. Mama had allowed herself to be tempted by the things that were illicit and illegal, but Esther knew that she never would. Oliver Moreland by all accounts lived on the edge of right, but slipped into the wrong as it suited him.

She wished that she could dismiss him without a backward glance, but she could not, and that admission only brought more dread and dismay.

When she spoke with him she felt as if the person she never let out escaped, an honest person without the frayed edges of her past.

The evening was a long one, complete with dancing and a delicious dinner, the entertainment set up comprising a rural company of troubadours who were surprisingly good.

After their exchange in the hallway Oliver was left wondering just what it was that held him here. Esther had told him what she wanted for her life in no uncertain terms, a place in society and all that entailed. If he'd had any sense, he would have simply left her alone, but he did not want to.

He had danced with many of the women here except for Esther, who had been mostly in the company of Lord Alberton, her dress tonight one of a dark blue velvet embroidered in a silver thread and giving the impression of a traveller from the heavens.

She was easily the most beautiful woman in the room, the grace and bearing in everything she did so very noticeable. He couldn't remember that her mother had been the same at all, his recall of the woman he had picked up that long-ago night one only of reticence, fear and heaviness.

Perhaps Lady Duggan had instructed Esther on dignity, for the woman had a lot of it herself, though she frowned every time she looked upon him. The Barrington-Hall party was all together at one table on the other side of the room, Alberton and his parents included with them.

Barrett and he had been placed on the opposite corner and among many young women who were all watching them as if they were the next choice on the menu.

'If you were not here, Oliver, I'd be over sitting with Sarah, so you have much to thank me for.'

'I'll take my leave tomorrow, then, for I can see that it would be easier if I went.'

Barrett frowned. 'I believe the young women nearby would probably think differently. Besides, isn't it always good fun to confound the enemy?'

'How do you mean?'

'I am sure you must have noticed that Lady Duggan has you on her "be wary of" list. You need to cajole her into thinking otherwise if you want to have at least a word with her beautiful niece.'

'And how do you imagine I might do that?'

'Use your charm. You are rich, after all, and even she must see the way Alberton rattles on about horses all the time when he is not extolling his farm-related money-making schemes.'

Esther and Alberton were heading again towards the dance floor.

Were they a couple now?

That thought had Oliver walking across to where Miss Priscilla Tompkins was sitting with a group of her friends, and he asked her to dance.

Rising immediately, she placed her hand across his arm, her hair catching the light as she moved, the dark of it enhanced by other colours of red and russet and ebony.

Much later he was standing by the large windows to one end of the room when Esther unexpectedly joined him. He had no idea where Alberton had got to, but was pleased for his absence.

'A fine evening,' he said and she nodded. He kept his tone formal because eyes were undoubtedly upon them, but her continued silence worried him, because more usually she had plenty to say.

'Barrett Brooker is very enamoured with your cousin.'

She glanced behind them at the group on the other side of the room. 'Sarah deserves a good man. I hope he is that.'

'He is.'

'A loyal man? A moral man? One cannot expect perfect, of course…' He got the feeling that she'd wished to say more, but had decided against it.

'Barrett is an interesting conversationalist, at least, and his world view is fashioned from experience and expedience.'

'You are referring again to Lord Alberton in your comparisons?'

'It is hard not to point out the differences.' He stopped there, feeling petty suddenly.

'I should imagine a man who makes it a point to flirt with every woman in the room has not the high ground to throw stones, so to speak, Mr Moreland. Faults come in all shapes and sizes.'

He laughed because he could not help it and because he liked her feistiness. 'Your aunt finally seems to have warmed to me, at least.'

She moved closer, the storm clouds in her eyes riveting. 'Why on earth would you be worried about that?'

'She seems to have much sway over you.'

'I don't understand…'

'I want you to like me, Esther, or at least to see beyond my reputation.'

Her mouth fell open and to an extent so did his own. Why the hell had he just said that? Was he drunk or addled? Had she bewitched him in some way like the sirens on the rocks had enticed Odysseus in the Bay of Capri? Heavy footsteps had them both turning and Alberton was there, a look of fury nestled in with cold hard humour on his face. Oliver could smell strong drink on his breath.

'Miss Barrington-Hall is about to dance with me, Moreland. We have an agreement between us and I would prefer it if you were to leave her alone.'

'Would you?' He took a step back because reasoning with a drunk was unwise, but as he turned to bid Esther goodnight Alberton hit him, right on the side of the nose with a quick, clear whack. He heard the crack of it even as he fell, blood spurting on to the patterned Aubusson rug beneath his feet. He couldn't get up because he felt dizzy, the sound of his heart beating loud in his ears. He'd hit his head on an edge of wood as he had fallen—the side of a table, perhaps, or a chair? He swore roundly as he tried to sit and heard the intake of breath from all those around him.

Someone was shouting from the doorway now, urgently and with vigour. Not Barrett because he was kneeling beside him, trying to get him up. No, it was Benjamin Barrington-Hall, and although he came towards him taking long strides, he was not quite on the right trajectory.

Esther. She was swaying beside him in her star-spangled dress, her eyes wide and her hands shaking. He wanted to stand and reach up, but he couldn't, his world still blurred and unreal.

Esther. Had he said it? Had she heard?

Her oldest cousin simply stooped to pick her up, like a doll, weightless, and her head lolled back as he took her from the room, leaving them all to watch.

'Get out, Moreland. Leave this house.'

Alberton's voice crashed back into his consciousness, a booming resounding anger in every single word, hands fisted again as if another strike was imminent.

Then Sarah Barrington-Hall was there between them, clinging on to Barrett, telling him to go, too, before things became worse.

And they were outside, a carriage with horses and two footmen and the wind everywhere. Had he fainted somewhere in between? Had he lost so much blood reality was waning?

'You will be all right, Oliver.' Barrett's voice. 'You'll be all right once we get out of here.' The curious panic in his voice was not reassuring. 'I'll find a doctor.'

Then he was in a room he did not recognise, a small room with candles burning and the smell of ammonia close. Another gap in time? He thought he should be alarmed, but the emotion was too hard to reach for so he just lay there.

'Ah, you are finally awake. That is good.'

A small balding man dressed in brown tweed sat before him, a stethoscope around his neck and glasses balanced across his nose. 'What is your name?'

He couldn't remember.

'What year is it?'

He could not remember that, either.

'Do you know this man?' He pointed to Barrett.

'My...friend.'

'Well, that is some improvement at least.' The

stranger's hand came to his temple. 'You have been hurt, Mr Moreland.'

'Hurt?' Nothing made sense.

'You hit your head. I think you have a concussion.'

The physician stood and gathered a hand mirror from the top of a cabinet, bringing it across and holding it before him.

His hair and nose were bloodied, but it was the raised knotted lump of skin at his temple that caught his attention.

'An inch higher and you would undoubtedly be dead.'

Oliver shut his eyes, no longer willing to look, and welcomed the dark as nausea came in waves upon him.

She was shaking and shaking and could not seem to stop.

'Get another blanket,' her aunt ordered and Sarah rushed to pluck one from the cupboard. 'And shut the door. Don't let anyone in and, Charlotte, stop crying for it is getting on my nerves.'

'Will Esther be…all right?'

'Of course she will. It is just a passing thing.'

Esther wanted to believe her aunt, for the worst was over, she knew that it was, but her attacks of panic always followed a precise pattern and she had to wait until all the stages were dealt with.

It was the blood, she thought, all over Oliver Moreland's face and in his hair, the dark gash of injury at his temple swelling as she watched. Just like her mother's had…

She gasped and held on to Aunt Mary's hand more tightly.

'It will pass, my darling. Let it go, remember. Don't try to hold it in. Let it flow out from you and away.'

Like a river. Like a stream. Falling through her. The image of such an idea always calmed her, a dark, hidden and quiet place to be.

Her world was reforming, the small pieces of it finding a whole, her breath deepening, too, and the ache of horror becoming more distant.

Where was Oliver Moreland now? Was he still here at the Beaumonts' house? No one had looked very pleased with him and Alberton had acted positively vilely. She hoped he would not come to visit her here in her room. She hoped they could leave as soon as she was better. The weight of her worry was making it hard to breathe.

'Put your head between your legs, my dear.' Her aunt was pressing her into that position. 'There. That is good.'

Benjamin was sitting on the other side of the room, looking concerned, and her aunt addressed him.

'We will leave in the morning, Ben, as I think the Beaumonts need some space to themselves. As for you, Esther, it would be best not to encourage any other suitor for a while until we sort this all out.'

'Sort it out?' Sarah asked in a tone that was furious.

'Obviously Alberton acted badly as did Mr Moreland. He is a guest here and it is more than evident that Lord Alberton was courting Esther. He should not have been speaking to her alone as he was and away from the others. He ought to simply have left her to enjoy the adulation she was plainly receiving from the only son of this estate.'

'My goodness, Mama, times have changed since you were a girl and they were well within sight. I hardly think Oliver Moreland deserved the treatment Lord Alberton meted out.'

'Well, my dear, let us look at this another way. Too many incidents like this and Esther's reputation will be in tatters. She will be thought of badly if she is not careful, a woman who inspires young men to act foolishly and rashly and ignore the tenets of proper behaviour.' Aunt Mary's words struck terror in Esther.

Like her mother. Men could never leave Alexandra alone, either.

Oliver Moreland was hardly to be compared to those men, though. All he had said was he had wanted her to like him and he had never intimated anything improper.

But her aunt was right, too. It did not take much of a scandal to propel one into a world that was not safe.

Breathing in she found her first words.

'I…want to go…home.'

'And you shall, my love. We will leave first thing in the morning for London.'

He woke to the world in the morning light, lying in a bed he did not recognise and a place he did not know, all the small bits of his memory reformed into a whole.

Esther.

She had fallen down and her cousin had caught her, but not before he had seen the horror on her face, just another layer of mystery surrounding her.

She never quite did what he expected and her cousin's expression had shown the sort of worry that came with old wounds and past problems.

He had said that he wanted her to like him just before Alberton had turned up with his fury and clenched fists. Was Esther with him now, ruminating on that awkward confession as she allowed the son of the house to comfort her? An agreement, he had said, that was between them? Could Alberton have already elicited a promise of something permanent from Esther?

From his point of view, the whole evening had been a disaster. He'd had a few seconds with her after dancing with every other eligible girl in the room and had said things that she obviously had no wish at all to hear.

A lost chance which had now left him with a broken nose, a gash across his temple and a headache that had no intention of abating.

He wished he was home, in his town house away from everyone, locked up in the solitude he so badly needed to heal.

God, he was lurching from accident to accident with an increasing tempo and at this rate would hardly be alive for very much longer. His side hurt, his eyesight was blurred, his nose was aching and his head felt strange. That was not even taking into account the lingering wound on his left leg where Merlin had scraped him against the fence or the gash at his temple.

Seminal moments in life came rarely and Esther Barrington-Hall had been present at a few of the most important ones. The trip to Camden Town through a snowy night. His distress in the quadrille at the Keegan ball. His pledge to himself not to interfere with Alberton's pursuit of her. Turning points. Signposts to live differently.

He would return to London, but stay out of society— it was the only sensible thing that he could do. He needed to leave her to live a calm, safe life, the kind she had told him she wanted after such a difficult upbringing.

Another thought hit him then. Had the blood from his head wound reminded her of some moment with her mother, a moment that had thrown her back into the chaos?

Closing his eyes, he breathed in, trying to find calmness. Esther Barrington-Hall was not for him and he needed to find the courage to truly believe that.

He had saved her once by taking her with him, but now he would save her for the second time by letting her go, unbeknown to her maybe, but every bit as important as the first.

Such thoughts reassured him and when the door opened and Barrett stood there, he managed to smile.

'You are looking better, Oliver, and the doctor will be pleased.'

'Where are we?'

'My country estate for I could not think where else to bring you at so late an hour in your condition.

The physician will be back this morning after which I shall return you home.'

'Thank you. I am sorry for…all this.'

Barrett brushed his apology away. 'Alberton had no cause to do what he did. I think the man is a menace and I hope Miss Esther Barrington-Hall decides the same thing.'

'She fell? I saw her there.'

'She did, though Sarah sent a note this morning to say that her cousin was a lot better and that they would be returning to London.'

'She knows where we are?'

'I left a letter for Sarah as I could see you were in no condition for a long journey. Perhaps it might be a good idea to lie low for a while? Give yourself a chance to recover?'

'I was thinking the same thing.'

'Esther Barrington-Hall looks to have her share of secrets, too, and her demons. How the hell do you know her, Oliver, for I sense there is some history between you?'

'I gave her and her mother a ride years ago when they were trying to leave London. Her mother was a woman who was more than down on her luck.'

'That's why they protect her, then, all the Barrington-Halls. Sarah said something about her being…hurt.'

'I think she is a lot stronger than she appears to be.'

'And last night?'

'Was a mistake. I should not have approached her.'

Barrett began to laugh. 'I can't believe you mean that. You who have always taken every risk in the book for countless years and with myriad women and got away with it?'

'Perhaps there is a time when risks do not pay off, some chance and probability equation that means one cannot succeed for ever.'

'You sound better. More like yourself.'

'I am. Let's forget about the doctor and go back to London. I just want to be home.'

'I want you to like me.'

These little words went round and round in Esther's head as she sat in the carriage with her aunt and uncle as they made their way back to the city.

Oliver Moreland had not needed to say anything, but plainly he had wanted to, though she was not sure just exactly what he had meant.

Lord Alberton had come to see her off, full of apology and explanation, and she had listened to him politely even while deciding that she did not wish to ever see him again. Her aunt had been more forgiving, advising her to place some time after the 'little incident' so that she might put things into a proper order. She had not mentioned Mr Moreland at all, though she had certainly sung the praises of Lord and Lady Beaumont and their beautiful estate.

'Never marry for convenience, Esther, or for love.' Her mother's words the day before she had died. *'Your father and I made that mistake between us so promise me that you will find a man who will let you be exactly who you want to be.'*

The little girl she had been had promised, hand

across her heart and tears in her eyes, because for a good month her mother had been largely under the influence of some drug that had made her distant and confused and this was the first time she had spoken with any clarity.

But the words implied Alexandra had had personal experience of such a choice and for the hundredth time Esther wished her mother had explained things about her father, explained their relationship, explained their problems.

The same caution that had been in her mother's eyes was also in her aunt's. Aunt Mary wanted her to be happy, Esther was sure of it, but she also wanted her to marry appropriately in order to be happy.

Sarah had come to see her and she had been adamant that Mr Brooker would be looking after Oliver Moreland.

'I am sure they will both be back in London, for I know they stayed at Mr Brooker's country estate last evening which already gives them a head start. Oliver Moreland certainly seems accident-prone, does he not, though it was hardly his fault this time for Alberton's behaviour was simply abysmal. Did Lord Alberton think you were flirting with Mr Moreland? What a ridiculous assumption, for I cannot see you with a suitor so unmatched in a thousand years.'

Unmatched.

The word made Esther frown.

She liked talking to Oliver Moreland. She'd liked dancing with him as well. She enjoyed watching him across a crowded room, watching him smile. She loved the colour of his eyes and the way her hand felt in his when he had reached out and taken it. She liked his honesty and his bravery and the history that wove them together even as it tore them apart.

Lord Alberton was a fine match according to everyone and all Esther could see of him was a lord who had never had to fight for anything, a man who expected all his wants to be met. A shallow man of little import. A man who would dismiss others because they were less wealthy, less lucky and less greedy.

These thoughts had her taking in breath for she could not quite understand their meaning. But Sarah was not finished.

'Mr Moreland has been on and off with Lady Winifred Leggett for a year or so now. She has her own detractors, given her wildness, but on all accounts they make a well-suited couple.'

'Do they?' Esther could not help voicing her question.

'Lady Winifred has had her fair share of suitors and there are rumours about her that are not quite exemplary. Much the same as Oliver Moreland's, I would guess, and at twenty-five she must be feeling some urgency to settle down. They have a veritable fortune between them so they will be more than secure.'

Perhaps such a fate was one Oliver Moreland wanted, Esther thought, a wealthy titled bride and a bunch of children who might inherit the riches of his family. A place in society that was set in tradition and all prior sins absolved.

There was some comfort in conforming after all,

a relief of coming in from the wilderness. Of all the people in the world she was the one to most know that.

But her horizons had dimmed a little, the possibilities of what her life might have been like waning. Alberton was gone as a suitor and she was pleased for that, but she could not imagine going back into the fray of the Marriage Mart again.

Perhaps she was destined to be alone? If her mother had never married, Esther was sure Alexandra's life would have been infinitely better. She knew nothing of her mother's family for Alexandra had refused to speak of them. All she did know of her grandparents on her mother's side was that they had passed away many years ago and that her mother had never felt close to them.

A sad tale and a cautionary one. Her father's family was all that stood between what had happened to Alexandra happening to her and she needed to be careful that they were not disappointed in who she became.

The world was a large and dangerous place, and if Oliver Moreland had made it temporarily a more delightful one she knew instinctively that it would not have lasted.

He had his life and she had hers and a chance meeting years ago when he had helped her, helped them, was not to be confused with expecting more.

'I want you to like me, Esther. To at least see beyond my reputation.'

She wished he had not said these words. She

wished he had said nothing because hope was a hard road to travel after suffering the sort of childhood she had.

But her anxiety had lessened its hold and Esther had been glad when the Barrington-Hall party had finally been ushered into two conveyances and driven away from Grafton Manor.

Chapter Six

Oliver used the next few weeks to strengthen his position in the affairs of the St Mary's Home he contributed to in Whitechapel. He barely went back into society and, apart from Freddie, Barrett, Michael and Julia, he saw nobody.

He walked each day in Hyde Park, but very early, early enough to miss most of those who also used the green spaces, because he needed a break from the society he had been in for so long and which defined him in a way that was no longer appropriate.

It was the sins of a wild youth come back to haunt him, he supposed, but lately he felt as if his life was going on a different track, one with charity and benevolence as a cornerstone of his intentions.

He had not slept with a woman in weeks, the thought of bedding anyone except for…

This line of thought was shocking and he stood stock-still. Except for Esther Barrington-Hall. There, it was admitted, the cold, hard fact of his need for her, worrying and impossible. He felt marooned on some sort of endless ocean, like the Coleridge poem he remembered from school and had always liked, the one about the sailor who had shot the albatross and been segregated from polite society ever since, the unwanted guest at a wedding whom no one truly understood.

His sins were of wildness and of a dissolute lifestyle. With no family to anchor him he had done as he willed for years, spinning out of control, all the character traits that now kept him from approaching Esther, her family shielding her from anyone whom they deemed unsuitable. This was his penance and his punishment. If the world in England was balanced on the scales of fairness, there was probably some justice in that, too. Had he not had money and some standing he would have been thrown out of society years ago and that was no small admission. He had failed in life just as his mother and father had, and his brother. All unbalanced and unrepentant. His work in Whitechapel was the only part of his life that was good and whole and honourable, and he meant to keep helping those less fortunate than himself until his very last breath.

On the thirteenth day after leaving the Beaumont house party he saw Esther Barrington-Hall and her cousin Charlotte coming towards him, two maids in tow behind and all well wrapped against the brisk northerly that had swept into the city.

Esther wore a burgundy velvet coat, her matching bonnet pulled down hard against the wind, her blonde hair showing beneath in an elaborate plaited loop and tethered firmly with pins.

'Mr Moreland,' Charlotte Barrington-Hall said and her smile was wide. 'It is good to see you so recovered.'

He smiled back. 'Indeed I am, Miss Charlotte, and not before time.'

Esther's green eyes observed him closely. Shock was there and worry. Charlotte Barrington-Hall had turned to talk with one of the following servants, who had asked a question, and the action allowed them a small space of privacy.

'Sarah said that your friend Mr Brooker had taken you to his estate, so you probably returned to London at about the same time as I did.' Her voice was soft, though there were lines of concern across her brow. 'You still have a scar. There.' Her fingers touched the skin of her own temple and he smiled.

'One of many,' he returned, wondering why he had said that even as he did so because the words only underlined his jeopardy. But Esther made him clumsy, ham-fisted even, his more normal polish disappearing under her green gaze, the distance he usually held on to with such tenacity washed away like some feeble thing.

'I am sorry about Lord Alberton—'

He interrupted her. 'The man's poor manners are hardly your fault.'

Charlotte was beside Esther now and he stepped back a little, the wind off the river cold on his face.

'You do not ride this morning, Mr Moreland. I

should have liked to have seen your steed up close. A thoroughbred, is it not? Why, I imagine its name and pedigree are listed in the General Stud Book, and how wonderful it must be to own an animal of such magnificence.'

'You are well informed, Miss Charlotte, but then I had heard you have a fine love for the equestrian.'

'I do indeed, though Alberton cured me of the trait somewhat when we were in his company for a long four days.'

'His passion around horses runs high.'

'You allow him more grace than we do, Mr Moreland.'

He looked straight at Esther then and saw a gentle frown run into her brow, but when she did not comment further he tipped his hat and watched them walk on.

Damn. Damn. Damn. The single word ran around and around in Esther's head as Charlotte's arm threaded through her own.

'You are quiet, Esther? Do you not think Oliver Moreland the most beautiful man who ever lived and was it not unexpected to meet him here so early in the morning? Why, I should have imagined him to be abed till at least noon and in the company of some scintillating opera singer or lady of the night. Both exceedingly well endowed, of course, and most enamoured by him.'

'I think your imagination is running away with you, Charlotte, for I should certainly not be thinking of any such thing.'

'Is it not hard sometimes, Esther, to stick to the rules with such exactness? You could have any man you wish in society and you know it and yet you choose to have none of them. Mama said the other day that you need to be making up your mind about a spectacular marriage while you can, for the second Season is harder than the first for any woman, no matter how well she looks, and I can assure you from my own wretched experience that she is correct.'

'Sarah seems to have found exactly the man she desires and this is her second Season?'

'Unbelievably you are right and any day now I hope she will say yes to Mr Brooker's proposal.'

'He has asked her to marry him?'

'She says so.'

'But she hasn't agreed?'

'She worries for us, I think. She worries we might both be harangued into an alliance that will be un-fulfilling and we will be sad for all of our lives. A woman's happiness, she stresses, is completely de-pendent on the quality of the man she weds.'

'She thinks your mother will force us into unions we do not wish if she is not there?'

'Society has its demands. Surely you understand that, Esther? Mama only wants the very best for us. It's not as if she would agree to wedding us off to a monster or to someone extremely old or poor.'

The truth of what her cousin was saying was like a sting. She would be expected to choose and the one man that she felt anything for was completely unavail-able to her.

She wished suddenly and desperately that she could simply go back in time, back to when Oliver Moreland had told her that he wanted her to like him.

Because she did like him, more than like him, and she could never say anything about such feelings to anyone.

Looking around, she saw him striding on in the other direction, away from her, the wind in his coattails, the sun on his hair.

Lord Alberton had sent her myriad messages, each one more fraught than the one before, and she had answered none of them. At the balls since, she had acknowledged him, allowing him the obligatory one dance, but nothing else.

Oliver Moreland hadn't turned up to any event that she had attended. She had seen his friends Mr Bronson and Mr Brooker once or twice but they had not approached her, either.

No, hers was a silent, secret attraction, an unreturned regard that was both foolish and heartbreaking. If she had any sense, she would move on, but she couldn't.

Wouldn't.

Such a thought brought back the many shades of her mother's personality, a woman who was so stubborn in her desperation that she had lost sight of reason. Esther tried to smile even as she questioned why her life was so impossible to live well.

On their return home the house was alight with a joyous celebration.

'Sarah is to be married, girls, for she has just in-

formed us that she has said yes to the wonderful Mr
Brooker. Your father knew of his intentions, of course,
but he said nothing at all to me and so it has come as
a most magnificent shock.'

Sarah herself was standing next to Aunt Mary and
she did look particularly radiant at her mother's enthusiasm, the ring she had on the fourth finger of
her left hand a large diamond surrounded by smaller
blue sapphires.

'We are going to have a party here in a month to
celebrate the occasion. Mr Brooker has his list of
friends and Sarah and your uncle and I have ours. If
there is one particular person you would like to add
to our list, girls, I would be pleased to know of it.'

Charlotte instantly gave the name of a friend of
hers, but Esther shook her head. Would Mr Moreland be on Barrett Brooker's list? Surely he would?

'We will have new gowns made for the occasion
as we need to appear at our very best. The Brookers
are an old and wealthy family so we must be up to
snuff, so to speak. We will invite everyone and open
up all the downstairs salons and goodness knows it
has been an age since we last had a grand party here.
Even Thomas is looking forward to it and that is saying something.'

As Charlotte and her mother wandered off on to
another topic Sarah took the opportunity to pull Esther to one side.

'I hope you would not be averse to our inviting Mr
Moreland, Esther? I don't care if Mother is unhappy,

but I did want to make sure that you were aware he might come.'

'Of course he should. He is a special friend of Mr Brooker's, is he not?'

'His closest friend, probably. It is just that after the trouble at Alberton's house party I wondered perhaps…' She stopped.

'Wondered what?' Esther's voice shook slightly as she asked this.

'I had wondered if you might have a firm opinion of Oliver Moreland one way or another. Barrett says that he is hard to read sometimes and might give impressions that are not always favourable—'

Esther did not let Sarah finish. 'No, not at all. I think Mr Brooker should invite whomever he wants.'

'And you, Esther—who do you want?'

'After the debacle with Lord Alberton I wish for nobody at all.'

Sarah laughed. 'Well, you are young and in your first Season, Esther. We will see if you feel the same by the end of it.'

Ben and Aiden's arrival brought them back to the others and Esther was pleased that Sarah's forthcoming nuptials had led to such joviality given the awful ending to the Alberton house party. Pushing down worry, she went to join her family.

Oliver knocked on the door with all the force of fury, the dingy and fetid surrounds of Goulston Street in Whitechapel adding to his anger. When the man he knew as Todd Blackburn answered, it was all he could do not to punch the fellow hard in the face so he would know the pain of a beating in much the same way Tobias Grant must have known it a few days before.

Instead he reined in his temper and took in a breath.

'If you as much as touch a hair on Tobias Grant's head again, I will have you beaten to within an inch of your life. Do I make myself clear? I have both the money and connections, Mr Blackburn, but more importantly I have the will to hurt you badly. And I shall.'

The man opposite stepped back, all fight gone. 'It weren't me, sir...'

'I don't care who it was. The boy was in your care and you did not protect him.'

He felt the presence of another behind him then, the malevolence almost palpable, and when an arm came out just as he expected it to he had the wrist in his grip, bending it with force, the newcomer going down squealing like a pig.

'Next time I won't be as kind,' he said then. 'Do we understand each other?'

The commotion had attracted a group from the nearby houses, ill-clothed wraiths and vagabonds with the sort of fear on their faces that came from a thousand days of hunger.

Hell, he could not save them all. One at a time, he had promised himself, one at a time starting from the very youngest up and Tobias Grant was a small and timid five-year-old, who had not deserved the brutal hiding Blackburn had given him.

If they hated him, it helped, but if they feared him, then that was even better. One did not live long in Whitechapel without some semblance of violence and his particular type of it was backed up by three years of stamping his mark upon the place.

People here knew he did not jest, they knew he meant what he said and they also knew that there were enough people in the low streets of desperation who supported his attempts to help the forgotten children.

With intent he turned towards the melee behind him and eyed them up, pleased when a gap opened and he walked on through. It took more energy than these wretched souls possessed to fight and they knew it, instead conserving what they had for the search of the next meal.

He hoped Esther had not ever seen this side of life as a young girl with her mother, but something told him that she probably had and his fists bunched at his side.

Barrett was waiting for him in his library when he returned home half an hour later.

'You have been in Whitechapel again?' His friend's glance took in the dark plainness of his dress.

'I have. A young boy was beaten up badly and I went to make sure the perpetrator never does the same again.'

'A difficult task, by the looks.'

'But a necessary one. What brings you here so late in the evening?'

'I'm to be married, Oliver. Miss Sarah Barrington-Hall said yes to me this afternoon.'

'So you have broken out the brandy? I hope you chose an expensive bottle.'

Barrett turned the label around. 'A Croizet B. Léon Cognac from the Comet Vintage of 1811. A good omen, I think, because I am here to ask you to be my best man, Oliver.'

He felt a short, sharp delight at the idea. 'I would be honoured to.'

'Sarah will no doubt employ her sister, Charlotte, and her cousin, Esther, as her attendants.'

Another shot of joy passed through him.

'And where will the ceremony be held?'

'We thought to hold it at the small Anglican church in Kensington in a few months, though the Barrington-Halls have spoken of their desire to put on an elaborate affair as a prelude to the occasion, an engagement party, so to speak.'

'I am pleased for you both, for Sarah is a woman of good sense, beauty and intelligence and will do you well, Barrett. Where will you live when you are married?'

'At Kingston Manor. I am leaving the Home Office for good, for intelligence is a young single man's game and I have been wearying of it for a while now.'

'Let's drink to the future, then. To your health, happiness and the country life.'

Oliver took the glass that Barrett had poured for him and downed the lot.

'Remember when we used to drink poorer versions of cognac glass after glass, Oliver?'

'And suffer the next morning for it. Have you told Freddie of your plans?'

'Not yet, for he is out of town till next week.'

'Out of town? He did not say?'

'You have been too busy recuperating from your accidents and he did not wish to turn your mind from the healing. He has met a woman in Exeter and is besotted. She is a woman of trade, a shopkeeper it seems, who holds a healthy share of the flower business in that city.'

Oliver began to laugh. 'Good on him.'

'He might bring her to the wedding.'

'Even better.'

'His parents are not pleased.'

'They were generally never pleased with anything, but, despite them not wanting it to, the world is changing and becoming fairer for those with less fortune.'

'And you have just returned from trying to sort that out?'

You were always good at detail, Barrett.'

'And you have always favoured the underdog, Oliver.'

Barrett leant back against the chair he was sitting on, looking thoughtful. 'I want children. I want to see what sort of parent I can be.'

'A good one, I am sure of it, for you've parents who showed you the way of it with ease and grace.'

Sipping at his brandy, Oliver thought of his own parents, a mother who was constantly despondent and a father who thought anger solved everything. New relationships had a way of making him maudlin, though thinking of Esther Barrington-Hall did not.

There it was again, that connection, that difference. He wished he might simply knock on the door of the town house in St James's Square and ask to see her.

He knew she was back in society and that she was undoubtedly the darling of the Season yet again. She deserved such adulation and regard because she was a good person who had overcome obstacles and triumphed. A person who should have all her dreams realised.

'You are lost in thought, Oliver?'

'It's been a long day.'

'You have not been out much of late. Everyone is asking where you are.'

'I think I am like you, Barrett. I need a different direction and a quieter life. Today in Whitechapel I realised that no matter how much you do to improve the lot of others, it will never be enough. It's not that I want to give up entirely, for I will continue with financial support of St Mary's Home, but I think I need to stop for a while. Get away. Recover.'

'Does this have anything to do with the person who shot at you and Michael in Hyde Park a month or so back?'

'Perhaps, for my fight against those who use children for their own means has garnered enemies.' He lifted his glass again. 'For now I want some peace,' he said simply.

'And happiness,' Barrett countered. 'God knows we deserve that.'

My mother felt that she did not, he almost said. Miranda had taken every small slight personally, blaming her problems on him and Phillip and their father. When she had drowned in the lake one afternoon in her thin nightgown the water had taken her down into the oblivion that she sought. Afterwards his father had found notes written to each of them, words of blame and reproach and condemnation.

Oliver had thrown his letter in the fire after the first read, but Phillip had kept his in the drawer next to his bed for years to be read again and again while trying to understand her accusations. He had no idea as to what his father had done for he had died a few years later after never mentioning his wife again.

Family. He did not know how a good one was supposed to work, a good one like the Barrington-Halls or the Barretts or even the Beaumonts, people who had made a template for conviviality and warmth. He wished that he did. He wished he could come in from the cold of his brother's resentment to form a relationship that was not so broken, the burden of brotherhood culminating in the bullet in his side from the gun held by Phillip.

Perhaps he had not meant to shoot him, but the fact was that he had and he had neither visited afterwards to make sure he'd survived nor apologised. To give Phillip his due, he'd had an affliction of tremors in his hands since birth.

'I have come to the conclusion that happiness needs to be sought.' Barrett's words made him smile.

'You will make a fine husband to Sarah and she will make you the same sort of wife, as you both are from solid families.'

'Whereas you are not?' The question was unexpected.

'My father was hardly a good husband and he was undoubtedly a poor parent after my mother simply gave up.'

'You told me about that little boy earlier on, the one beaten in Whitechapel. You handled that in the way my father would have and his father and the one before him. I think being a good man is more about knowing when to stand up for what is right and fighting for that. I think you have that inside of you, Oliver.'

'Perhaps.' He swallowed the rest of his cognac and poured himself another one. The doubt was still there.

'What made you decide Sarah was the one?'

Barrett laughed at the quick change of topic. 'I couldn't stop thinking about her. Everything I did had some sort of shadow with Sarah in it. She was just different.'

'Different?'

'Steadying. Honest.'

Oliver's life of late had been so up and down, with so many accidents and incidents that he felt unbalanced by it. He needed sturdy and steady and real. He needed what Barrett had found, a woman whom he could spend his life with and have children with and thrive.

Thrive. He smiled at the word for it was one he'd never thought of before as a foundation stone for his life.

'Your brother came to see me yesterday.'

Now this was new. Phillip was back in town?

'He asked me what he could do to make things right between you.'

'What did you say?'

'I said I did not know.'

'Well, that is the truth.'

'I also said that he should keep trying.'

'Fair enough.'

He left the topic there. So many things these days he did not want to think of or speak about and so many difficulties that he had not told Barrett or Freddie or Michael.

He put down his glass on the table before him.

'My mother left a note when she died for each of us. Mine said I would be just like her and never find happiness. I didn't ask Phillip what was in his, but I imagine it was something just as alarming.'

'God.'

'The sins of a parent visiting the children or whatever that saying is…'

'The sins of the father are to be laid upon the children. It's from Shakespeare.'

'And my father's sins did affect me.'

'Well, from what I knew of him he was always difficult. God knows how Phillip could stand to stay at Elmsworth.'

'My brother liked peace. He seldom rattled the chain.'

'Like you did?'

'Freddie once said he did not believe I was the Earl's son. Sometimes I did not believe it, either.'

'Well, with your father gone it's best to just leave that thought alone. Any divergence can only hurt you.'

Oliver nodded. 'Here's to marriage, then, and your beautiful bride, Barrett, for you deserve every happiness that comes your way.'

A week later Esther met Oliver Moreland again as she walked down Pall Mall with her maid in tow. He looked tall and solid and as beautiful as usual.

'You have not been in society much of late, Mr Moreland?' Esther began the conversation as he stopped before her.

'A prudent withdrawal, I think, given the last occasion that I was.'

'The Beaumont party?'

'Not my finest moment, I am afraid.'

'Nor mine, for I have never been particularly good around blood.'

'Well, everyone has their anxieties. I myself have an aversion to swimming in deep cold lakes and hence never do it.'

'A less likely fear to turn into a reality, though, don't you agree? People seem to bleed around me all the time and deep cold lakes are few and far between as well as easy to avoid. Are you better now?'

'Completely.'

He sounded distracted and Esther was unsure as to how to proceed. She chose a safe topic.

'My cousin Sarah said you are a close friend of Mr Brooker's. Have you known him for a long time, then?'

'Since we were sent to school together at ten years old.'

'Benjamin, my oldest cousin, said that you have many other loyal friends around you.'

'Which is a lucky thing given my recent troubles.'

He said this in a way that held honesty and humour and she liked him for it.

'There is usually a reason for such things, Mr Moreland.'

'I agree and family has a lot to do with it.'

Esther felt the blood rising in her cheeks. Did he refer to her past?

Today she felt out of step with him, all the things she wished to say stuck in her throat and unspoken. He was a stranger who walked through his world in a far different way from how she walked through hers. A man who broke rules and hearts and jaws and barely looked back as he did so. He had no close family, no constancy, no true ambition, either, to be anything other than what he was.

He lived carelessly and dangerously in the way Alexandra had and in a way that she herself would never choose to, not in a thousand years. Esther sought safety and shelter in the quiet corners of society, a place that protected those who did not stray. She was a woman of common sense and good judgement, traits that she clung to tenaciously because her childhood had contained so little of either.

No, the beautiful Oliver Moreland was not the man for her. She needed to be careful around him because under his dark blue glance things moved inside her breast and lower that had no business to be there.

Taking a breath, she smiled, feeling the stiff inflexibility of the emotion like a noose around her neck.

'I like rules and manners because from my experience these are the only things that keep the world from chaos.'

He laughed, but the sound was not kind.

'I cannot tell you what the secret of a successful life is, Miss Barrington-Hall, but I can tell you that a sure way to failure is to try to please everyone.'

'You think that is what I am doing?'

'Aren't you?'

This conversation had veered so widely from the one she had hoped to have with him, Esther was unsure as to which way to go from here. Still she took in breath and answered him

'Perhaps your way of pleasing no one has its flaws as well, Mr Moreland, for the illicit and the forbidden have their drawbacks.'

'Ah, but they are much more fun, Esther.'

Her name was said informally and in a tone that made her heart lurch. She was prepared for neither his wildness nor for his passion and he knew it.

Looking around, she was glad her maid still hung back, perusing the wares in the window of a chocolate shop, and so she took the chance.

'I think, sir, that we have probably come to the very edge of our patience with each other, but before you disappear altogether I would like to thank you for the confidentiality you have kept concerning my past. I have appreciated your silence.'

He laughed loudly. 'How little you know me, Miss Barrington-Hall.'

She frowned and stood her ground. 'Do you allow anyone to, or is it a rule of yours to send people off as soon as they might guess something that you may not wish them to know?'

He smiled in a way that was disconcerting. 'I've always found distance has its advantages because people can often be disappointing.'

Squaring her shoulders Esther answered him, 'Nothing hurts more than being disappointed by the one person who you thought would never hurt you.'

'Your mother?' Now he looked at her with more interest.

But she was not drawn into making a confession. 'After disappointment there comes hope and that is what I am focusing on.'

'Hope to make a good life? Hope for things to be better?'

'Yes, for without it one is lost and I have been.'

These words had him stepping back.

'I am sure things will improve markedly, Miss Barrington-Hall, for you are the belle of the Season with a choice of fine upstanding suitors who will do everything possible in their world to make your life a happy one.'

An impasse. An honesty. Words that put each of them in a place far from the other, but without blame attached.

She could see him retreat almost as a physical thing, a man who knew who he was and would never change. People had disappointed him, that much was for sure, but he had dealt with such frustration in an entirely different way from how she had. He had stopped trying to fit into expectations and walked a path that was far from her own.

The line of thoughtful suitors in society was growing around her just as he said, good men, easy men, men who would cherish and love her with all of their hearts. Undamaged men. Untouched by tragedy.

'I will see you at your cousin's wedding, then.' His words came through her musings. 'I am Barrett's best man and I heard you are to be one of the bridesmaids.'

And with that he was gone, lost into the throng of people on the busy street, only a glimpse of his height showing now and then in the widening distance as he walked, leaving Esther to wonder if she had done the right thing or the wrong one by burning such bridges.

Out of his company she felt the loss of what might have been. Once he had said to her that he wanted her to like him, but now...

The crashing waves of regret made her feel sick. Now they were each adrift on the edges of their preferences, hard lines drawn which precluded even friendship. Choices were not always easy, but life demanded them; she had learnt that very early on. She smiled as she spied Charlotte coming out of the haberdashery shop her cousin had gone into to explore a good fifteen minutes earlier.

'Was that Mr Moreland I saw out of the corner of my eye a moment or so ago, Esther?'

'Yes. He spoke to me briefly.'

'I thought so, for your colour is a few shades higher than it usually is.'

Esther did not reply to this as Charlotte took her arm.

'We will each find our own knight in shining armour soon, for any man would be lucky indeed to have us and as Sarah is a good year older we have plenty of time. She did not just jump at the first man offering his hand, but instead clung to the belief that the one she wanted to spend a lifetime with would come along. I want a man with a stable of fine horses and one who is generous and passably good-looking. What are your desires in a husband?'

'Kindness. Dependability. Steadfastness.'

Esther listed these things with barely any thought and knew to the very core of her that this was the truth of what she sought.

'Then Oliver Moreland is definitely off the books, dear Cousin, because he is none of those things.'

'You think I have considered him?'

'I am almost certain of it, Esther. You light up like a candle when he is around and I think Mama has noticed, too, and does not approve.'

'Well, do not worry, Charlotte, for I have no want at all to be in his company again.'

'Because you do not trust yourself?'

'Pardon?'

'You do not trust yourself not to break the rules you adhere to with such vehemence. You are also scared that your emotions will reign.'

Esther felt a fury well up. 'Maybe because I know what happens when they do.'

Charlotte merely raised her eyebrows. 'Your mother never loved my father's brother. That was what drove him to the drink because he loved her without reservation.'

'Who told you that?'

'Grandma before she died. She told me I was to protect you no matter what and I have tried with all my heart to do just that.'

The anger left Esther as quickly as it had come.

'And you have. You and Sarah have been like true sisters and I will be grateful for ever.'

'But it's not enough, is it?' Charlotte wasn't letting her off so lightly. 'It's not enough to simply follow instructions. Be this. Say that. Smile like you mean it. If I ever find someone who makes my heart beat as fast as Sarah's does for her Mr Brooker, I will follow such a feeling wherever it might take me because such a man may not come along twice.'

'You would follow your heart even if it might be dangerous?'

'To whom?'

'To you, of course.'

'How could it be so, Esther, for a shared love is not something to be measured in little pieces?'

'Has Sarah been telling you this?'

Charlotte blushed. 'Partly. But I know I will follow my dreams without hesitation.'

'Then you are lucky.'

As Esther said this she wondered if Charlotte had even heard her because she carried on.

'I saw Lord Alberton the other day and he asked me if you talk about him, for I think he would appreciate another chance at courting you. He does have wonderful horseflesh and his estate is magnificent and underneath he is not a bad man.'

'Well, that will not happen.'

'Because you don't give people a second chance?'

'No, because I never really gave him a first one and I have no interest whatsoever in the state of his stable.'

Charlotte began to laugh. 'My God, Esther, there are so many other men who stalk you at every available occasion and you don't even notice them. Mama is becoming increasingly worried for you.'

'She has Sarah to occupy her now. Benjamin told me last evening he was heaving a great sigh of relief because of it.'

'What else did Ben tell you?' Charlotte looked interested.

'He said if he marries before he is forty he would be surprised.'

'Forty? My goodness, if we left it that late we should never bear children.'

Children.

Esther turned the word on her tongue. She had never wanted the responsibility of being a parent after her childhood and that had not changed.

For a moment she felt as if all the parts of her life were colliding. The early days with her mother, her subsequent rescue and her introduction into a demanding society. Oliver Moreland had featured in some of these parts, by protecting her and making her feel safe.

He was not rigid like her, rooted in manners and protocol, and he was not scared, either. Take a chance, he'd said. Trust yourself and live.

Perhaps he was right.

She could not find a halfway point, a place where she might draw a line in the sand, a point where she could be happy. Though another thought came unbidden.

She might be happy with Oliver Moreland if she could only let herself.

Taking in a breath, she saw Charlotte watching her closely.

'Gambling is a part of life, Esther, and if you never risk anything you might miss out altogether. Mama counsels us to take the safe path, but Sarah didn't heed her advice and found love instead on her second Season. Imagine if she had married in haste.'

Like her mother. Alexandra had met her father one week and married him the next, much to the horror of his family. Mama had told this story again and again.

'Don't trust your heart, Esther. Promise me that if you ever do marry do it carefully and over time and never give your troth to a man whom you do not truly know.'

Well, she did not know Oliver Moreland at all.

She did not know his family or his beliefs. She did not know where he lived or what he did or how he managed his life.

She knew he was handsome and charismatic and wild, all shallow things that told her nothing. But she also knew that he had not betrayed her, had not gossiped, had not left her to deal with all the difficulties of anyone else knowing the truth of her past.

He was a puzzle and an enigma, a man whom people spoke of often and in so many different ways. Her cousins noted the loyalty of his friends and the gulf between the two brothers. Society spoke of his wealth and of his relationships with unsuitable women, fast women, experienced women. Aunt Mary could only see his wildness and his violence and Uncle Thomas his lack of morals, which was a shame because under this she had heard other things.

Sarah spoke of hidden work in the shadows among poverty and hopelessness, something she said that she had been told by Barrett Brooker, and Julia Buckley had been most complimentary of him at the Keegan ball.

A saint or a sinner? For the life of her Esther could not quite decide.

Chapter Seven

A note had arrived from his brother asking him to come to Elmsworth Manor for a meeting.

As this had never happened before Oliver was non-plussed. More usually there was no contact between them at all, but this letter held a certain difference, a pleading quality to it that was unusual. He wished he could have asked Freddie to come with him, or Barrett, but he knew both were busy. As a precaution he wrote a note to each of them and left it on the top of his desk just in case he did not return. He even toyed with the idea of writing to Esther Barrington-Hull to explain his absence just in case but decided against it.

The Elmsworth estate was as beautiful as it always had been when he arrived in the early afternoon, the late sun sinking behind the hills and the lake reflecting the sky. It had been a good year since he had last been here and although the place held hard memories, it still was home.

His brother was waiting in the library and Gretel, his wife, was standing beside him. Both were dressed formally.

Oliver tipped his head and waited as the door was shut behind the departing servant who had brought him through.

'Thank you for coming, Oliver. Last time things transpired between us that should not have and I realise that we have not been friends for years.'

Were we ever? He almost asked this question, but there was something about his brother's demeanour today that stopped him.

When a drink was offered he took it, relieved when they sat on two of the three chairs facing the blazing fire and asked him to do the same. Surely he would be safe with them all sitting down?

'You are no doubt wondering what this invitation is about?'

'Indeed I am.'

'I have asked you here because Gretel and I wish to leave Elmsworth Manor in the near future and travel to the Americas.'

These words jolted him back into the moment.

'To live? What of your life here?'

He noticed Gretel wipe away a tear with a dainty lace handkerchief embroidered in pink roses. A moment frozen in time that he would remember in detail for ever.

'We do not fit in here any longer and without the ability to provide heirs the place is in jeopardy. Gretel wants to see her parents in Richmond, Virginia. Without children...' He stopped and took in a breath and

Oliver heard the quiver in it. 'Without heirs this place has no future, so I am hoping...' He stopped again.

'That I will provide them?' Oliver finished the sentence.

He remembered his brother and him learning to ride together. He also remembered running across the fields in summer with the sun and wind in their faces after their father had strapped them yet again for some small infraction, laughing as they went.

When had they lost one another? When had it all changed?

After their mother had died, he supposed, and Papa had become an angrier man than before, drink providing him with some relief.

But Phillip was not finished. 'Before we go, however, I feel that I need to tell you I did not mean for the gun to go off last year. I only wanted to frighten you into realising that you were harming Elmsworth and the family heritage. I wanted you to understand that such privilege required sacrifice.'

'The sacrifice of my life?'

Unexpectedly Phillip began to laugh. 'You always overstated things, Oliver.'

'And you always had a hot temper.'

For just a second Phillip had the grace to look abashed. 'I am sorry.'

'For once I do believe you are.'

'Good. Now can I give you some advice? From one brother to another?'

Phillip waited till he nodded.

'Marry and be happy. Marry a wife like I have who

will teach you how to truly love. Our parents never knew the trick of that and it has showed for a long time in the both of us.'

Oliver shook his head because he did not want this discussion. Not like this. Gretel looked uncomfortable, too.

But Phillip continued. 'We leave England in a month. I need to be secure in the knowledge that Elmsworth Manor will carry on in safe hands. With heirs and a future. Your liaisons with women of dubious reputation have caused friction between us for years. If you continue with such a precarious existence, the estate and title will be lost from our family, lost to our father's cousin, who has three strapping lads and a great want to be the new Earl. You are twenty-five, Oliver, and soon to be twenty-six. If you would do one thing to make Elmsworth safer, then let it be the act of choosing a suitable wife to lead the family name through the next decades.'

When Oliver looked over at Gretel he saw tears running down her cheeks in a steady stream. God, they meant it. He was being roped into the Marriage Mart the same way that the young girls who first came out in society were, with no choice, little time and a great wallop of uncertainty.

He did not like it one little bit, but he could see no way out, for if they truly meant to go he could not abandon Elmsworth.

His brother was unpopular in England, society largely shunning him. There had been rumours, too, of Gretel's desperation and he had seen that first-hand when she had come alone to London to proposition

him a year ago, to ask for him to sleep with her so
that she might provide Phillip with a child. He had refused, of course, but his brother had shot him a month
later and he had always wondered exactly what she
had told him about her proposal.

Still, to end it all like this hardly seemed like a
good idea.

'I am wealthy in my own right, Phillip, and I do
not love this estate as much as you. Go to America
by all means, but leave yourself a way of coming
back. I will watch over things until you know what
you want, but I won't be pressured into marriage or
into the provision of heirs.'

'It cannot be left empty.'

'And I cannot live here permanently.' His tone allowed for no argument and Phillip stayed silent. Their
roles had changed, Oliver thought then, his brother
more uncertain than he had been and nowhere near
as arrogant.

'Just till this time next year, then. Would you give
me a year?'

Hell, he was going to say yes because he knew
there were undercurrents here, things that his brother
was not telling him, darker things. His childhood had
at least taught him to be a rigorous barometer for the
crisis points of others.

Barrett's conversation also came back to him, too,
his friend's desire to change things and live in the
country. Perhaps this would work. Perhaps this was
also a way for him to leave London in a quick, sharp
break, a way out? For a year.

Phillip stood then and walked over to a small desk,

opening the drawer at the top and bringing out a thick leather book.

'There are things you should know, Oliver. Things I should have told you, but didn't.'

He left the book on the table beside him and sat down again.

'You want me to read it now?' He glanced at the many loose pages he could see spilling from the edges of the leather.

'No. But I want you to take the book with you to London. I want you to understand.'

'Are you well?'

He needed to ask this question before he went because a serious illness was the only thing he could think of that might make his brother act in this way.

Gretel glanced at him in shock.

'I am.'

He heard the catch in his brother's voice and knew at that moment it was not Phillip who was sick, but his wife.

Fear had a certain stillness and it was all around him, caught in the glances and in the words and in the very way they both sat on the edges of their chairs as if waiting for the truth to pounce.

He said nothing because he understood they would wish him not to, but his heartbeat quickened.

'When do you go?'

'We have a first-class cabin, leaving in the next few weeks.'

'The weather will be better then.' He heard himself say this through a fog, the small details of an easier passage so inconsequential against the unsaid dread.

When he left here today he might never see them again.

Phillip asked if he would like a drink, but he shook his head. He wanted to be gone, gone with the over-stuffed book and its explanations and away from the sadness of all that would never be.

He got back to Westminster two hours later, back to the bustle of the city and to the noise. Back to his apartment. It was a relief.

The book stared at him from its place on the table beside him, the soft yellow ribbon that bound it shut belying all that he imagined might be inside. Pouring himself a brandy, he took one deep sip and another and then, opening the leather cover, he began to read.

Uncle Thomas called Esther into his office after an afternoon soirée that they had all attended. As Aunt Mary trailed into the room behind her Esther sensed that they wanted to talk about something important.

Already she had a good idea as to what that might be.

Once sitting, Uncle Thomas came straight to the point.

'You realise, of course, my dear, the effect you have had on the young men in society? I have had suitors lining up ever since you came out and things have got more and more serious as time has moved on.'

He pushed a list over for her to see, a good many names of would-be suitors written upon the sheet. She recognised many, but others she had no recall of at all. Oliver Moreland's name was not on the list.

'It seems, my dear, that it might be prudent to begin to make a choice. Your aunt presses such a sentiment on me many times a day and perhaps she is right in her desire for you to select a man whom you could be happy with. I have looked into all of the families and there is not one that the Barrington-Hall name would be tarnished by. In fact, it is the very opposite, for they are all stellar candidates with honourable reputations and fine lineages, all things that would do both you and our family proud.'

Not willing to be a mere observer, her aunt leapt in next. 'Alberton is still very keen to take his suit further, Esther, and so is Lord Coulton. The wealth of both these families is unmatched and you would be very lucky to be among their ilk.'

'But we agreed, Mary, that it should be Esther's choice alone. Remember? We will not influence your selection, my dear. You have to decide which one of these suitors you could be happiest with in the state of Holy Matrimony.'

'But I do not wish for any of them.'

Silence sat alongside shock in the room.

'There will be no better time than now. One mistake or one error could cut this number in half, you realise that?'

A veiled warning from her aunt, but a real one.

'I do not love any of them.'

'We are not asking for that, Esther.' Her aunt was in full flight now. 'No, it is respect we are after and the ability of the man to keep you in the manner in which you are accustomed. It is the fact of a fine family bloodline reaching down through time that will enable you to produce heirs of substance. Surely you see that?'

Horror swept through her. She had known that, after all the time, money and effort her aunt and uncle had put into her debut, there would need to be a conclusion, but she had not imagined the axe to be falling so soon. Sarah and Charlotte had been given the grace of two Seasons, but she was a niece who did not have the luxury of the same.

She could not make a fuss, either. Her future was too precarious. She knew, of course, they would not just toss her out, and the choices she had before her were probably the best she was ever going to be offered.

Andrew Wilfred, Charles Smythe, Lord Coulton. They were all nice men who were courteous, well-mannered and kind. And this was only the first three of the twenty or so other names she could see written there in a long and careful list.

A lucky choice. A reasonable selection. Many other girls of the Season would have nowhere near the range of names and would have been thrilled with such a selection.

Pick one. Pick one. Pick one.

The words buzzed through her mind even as her fingers entwined on her lap, the hard grasp of them making certain that she did not bring a digit up and point.

'I am not sure…' She was careful with her words.

'Then ask Sarah or Charlotte for their advice, my

dear, or any one of the boys if you wish for further detail, but do not tarry. Each one of these men is a catch and other girls will be vying for their notice. If we could have some sort of an answer by the end of tomorrow, your uncle could start talking to them.'

'Tomorrow?'

'Or the next morning, Esther, if you need another night to sleep on it.'

She tried to smile as she picked up the list, folded it over twice and stuck it in the pocket of her new velvet jacket.

Her aunt and uncle meant the best for her. It was just how it worked. They wanted her to be happy and this was the only way in their minds that they thought she could be.

She would not show her cousins the names because she did not want advice on which one to choose. She loved none of them, she wanted none of them. Not one of them made her heart beat faster or her cheeks flush.

Lord Coulton asked her to dance the next evening at the Coulton ball. He was a shortish man with twinkling brown eyes and a wide smile. She knew his family slightly, his three sisters kind girls who did not gossip.

'I am supposing, Miss Barrington-Hall, that you do realise I have asked your uncle if I may court you. He was not averse to the idea.'

'Yes, he did mention it to me.'

'I know I am not that dashing variety of a man that young girls might hanker for—'

She didn't let him finish. 'That is not the kind I am after at all, Lord Coulton.'

'James,' he said, 'and I am glad to hear it. I am more of a country man who enjoys walking and fishing and gardening. I don't particularly like horses.'

She began to laugh. 'Neither do I.'

'There are times, too, when I tire of society and want nothing more than a return to Hertfordshire, where the family lands are. However, my father is pressing me to settle down as I am the heir to the title and estates of the Coultons and I have only three sisters.'

'A universal problem, here in society. Not the sisters, but settling down, I mean.'

He laughed loudly and she liked the sound. An easy man. A man whom she could grow to like. He was not arrogant like Lord Alberton, which was a huge relief.

'Your family is close, Miss Barrington-Hall, and so is my own. I think it important to maintain congenial relations with kin in order to have a happy life. Are you of the same opinion?'

She nodded. 'My cousins are like sisters and brothers and my aunt and uncle like parents. I lost my own mother and father early, you see.'

'I had heard that and I am sorry for it. As much as my family is sometimes rather trying, I cannot imagine life without them. Perhaps one day you might like to bring yours up to my family home to visit. We have a rather old manor house sitting on a thousand fertile acres and while it is not the most stately place, it is indeed solid.'

Solid. Like he was. She could already see herself there, on the lawns of the home, their families mixing not with the formality of the Beaumonts, but in a far more relaxed manner.

'Where were you brought up, Esther? May I call you that?'

'You may. I was raised in Kent at Redworth Manor. My father was Lord Duggan's youngest brother.'

'And your mother?'

'Her family was from up north, but her parents both died very soon after her marriage.'

Please don't ask any more questions, she thought then, but he didn't, concentrating on the dance steps instead. She could almost hear him counting the beat in his head and smiled.

Catching her humour, he smiled back. 'I am not well practised at this. In fact, I am almost as poor at dancing as I am at horse riding.'

A partner in life could not give you everything, Esther thought then, for dancing was one of her delights. She loved the sound of music and the feel of moving to it.

'One thing I am good at, though, is beekeeping. Up at Hertfordshire we have fifty hives that I maintain personally and the honey is better than anything I have ever tasted.'

'They don't sting you?'

'No. I have special clothing and use smoke to calm

them. Besides, there is a lot of mutual respect involved between us.'

He went on then to tell her of the intricacies of
beekeeping and the way of the hive, and when the
music stopped and he brought her to the side of the
room they kept talking. His subject was interesting
and humorous, and Esther thought she was learning
things just by listening to him.

She saw her uncle beam at her from one side of
the salon and knew that her aunt was watching as
well. A good match. A substantial estate. A refined
and distinguished family. She was soon to be twenty
and she knew that for her there would not be a second
Season. Alexandra had been whimsical and impulsive
and flighty. She had never settled, never been content
with things. There was always a better opportunity
just over her shoulder and she had dragged Esther
into uncertainty for years and years.

She would not be like that. She would choose a
man wisely and stick it out, through thick and thin,
through good and bad. She swore that she would and
any dreams of someone or something else needed to
be squashed down with fervour.

Unpredictability led to unhappiness. Random impulsive choices led to ruin.

Well, she would not make such a selection, no,
she would not.

When Lord Coulton asked her to dance with him
again, she gave him her hand and went towards the
floor gladly.

Chapter Eight

'Did you hear that Miss Esther Barrington-Hall is engaged to Lord Coulton?'

Barrett's question made Oliver stir and the ennui that had engulfed him after reading the many letters written by his family in the book his brother had given him shifted for the first time in two weeks.

'The union was announced yesterday at the Hammond ball. Coulton looked like a cat who had got the cream.'

He did not rise at all to Barrett's taunt.

'The Coulton family is as delighted as the groom, it seems. They are highly thought of and most upright. Alberton at least was passed over.'

'When is the wedding to be?'

'After mine. In three months.'

'A rushed affair.'

'Perhaps they do not wish to wait. I remember Coulton from school. He is neither stupid nor unkind. When I gave Esther Barrington-Hall my congratulations after the announcement she looked happy.'

'Good.'

'You mean that?'

'Why would I not?' He tried to keep anger from his words.

'Perhaps because you watch Esther Barrington-Hall as if she should be your own and you have done so from the first moment you ever saw her.'

'Are you a seer now, Barrett? A man who thinks to know the mind of others?'

'I am a friend, Oliver, and have been one for a very long time.'

'Then as a friend you know me well enough to also know that Esther should be with a suitor like Coulton. He is from a stable family, his reputation is spotless and he has almost as much money as I have.'

'God.' Barrett looked astonished. 'You think you would ruin her?'

Oliver breathed in, wishing this conversation would just stop. 'I do think that because I would.'

Barrett began to laugh. 'You are telling me you haven't come forward, because you think you are protecting her?'

'I am.'

Barrett stopped laughing instantly.

'How?'

'By letting her go. She does not need me. She needs a man who is steadfast, responsible and constant.'

'Which are all things I could say about you.'

Oliver felt his throat thicken. It was the nicest thing Barrett could have said, yet he did not believe it was true. Phillip's letters in the yellow-ribboned book also fed into his hesitancy, the truths there more damning than even he had always thought them.

'She should marry Coulton. He will suit her well. It will be a satisfactory union.'

Lifting his glass, he watched the light from the chandelier above through the brandy. 'So here is to Esther Barrington-Hall and Lord Coulton. May they live well and long and happily.' The sentiment sounded nothing like he wanted it to.

Barrett lifted his own glass. 'I've known you too long to believe you could mean that, but I also know you well enough to allow you some space. You have not been out in weeks. Are you well?'

'Very.'

'You don't sound it. It is being said that your brother and his wife are departing for the Americas on a prolonged holiday?'

'They are. I met him a few weeks ago at Elmsworth because he wants me to watch over the place while they are away.'

'Then relations have progressed between you, it seems.'

'They have.'

'Well, the complexities of family exist in every form you can imagine. As much as I love my own, the thought of living in each other's pockets makes me shudder. So you will go back there, to Hampshire?'

'I'm thinking of it. Perhaps a time in the country would be good for me, to clear my head, so to speak.'

'And to find your place.'

'That, too.'

'Sometimes we have to go back to go forward. Freddie told me that before he left to find his flower heiress and it stuck with me. The party put on by Sarah's parents to celebrate our wedding is next week so I hope you will come to that.'

'Of course.'

'It will be a joint affair for Lord and Lady Duggan, though, to celebrate the two betrothals together.'

'That makes sense.'

'You will be all right there?'

'Of course. Why would I not be?'

The party thrown by Aunt Mary and Uncle Thomas was a combined one, a joyous celebration of two betrothals.

James stood beside her after they had welcomed their guests, his smile kind. 'You look beautiful, Esther. Like a goddess from the old Greek tales. Too beautiful for me, really, but there you are. The princess and the frog.'

It was why she had chosen him from the list presented to her. He was not a man who pushed himself forward or expected a great amount of deep conversation. He was an easy companion and a loyal one and he said things to her in a genuine manner that were both sweet and kind.

She knew Oliver Moreland was near the minute he stepped into the room, not because she saw him but because she felt him there, a ripple of unrest stealing through her. James was at her side, telling the group some humorous tale about a fishing trip he had once enjoyed. When she raised her left hand to push back a tendril of hair the large diamond ring he had given her glinted.

Engaged.

The fingers on her other hand closed across the bauble. She had known that Oliver Moreland would come, of course she had. He was to be Mr Brooker's best man and he should be here, but…

No. She let go of that thought and concentrated on what was real.

Aunt Mary beamed at her, and Charlotte at her side squeezed her arm. Further afield others watched James and her, the new couple of society, all the stars aligning. Members of the Coulton family were splayed out around them, too, listening in fondness to a story Esther thought had probably been told by James in the same way a hundred times before.

A favoured son. A brother and a grandson. Lord Coulton stood at the very centre of his family, a man of place and position.

She was lucky he had chosen her. She was fortunate in his steadiness and reliability and his placid disposition. It would be enough.

'You look lost in thought, Esther,' Charlotte said in a questioning way. 'Is not the evening a wonderful one? Two engagements and two weddings and all at once. I have never seen Mama and Papa look so happy or this room more alive and alight. I am just so pleased for you and for Sarah and I do so hope that before long it will be me standing here with a ring on my finger, too.'

Esther could not help but laugh, Charlotte's enthusiasm so endearing.

'Perhaps there is someone here already, Charlotte, and you just need to meet him?'

As they both looked around Esther caught the glance of Oliver Moreland and looked away, her courage besieged for a moment by another emotion. He had the most striking woman in the world on his arm, her golden dress floating around her.

'Oh, my goodness, but Mr Moreland has brought Lady Winifred with him tonight. Is she not exquisite?' As if remembering the place and occasion she then took back her words. 'I mean, you and Sarah look wonderful, too…'

Esther stopped her. 'Anyone can see how perfectly beautiful Mr Moreland and his partner appear together, Charlotte.'

'And imagine what their children might look like were they to wed?' Charlotte turned then and watched them again. 'Oh, they are coming over here with Mr Brooker. I would guess they wish to give you their congratulations.'

Dread simply drained into Esther and to steady herself she placed her hand on James's arm, liking the sturdiness of the touch.

'Miss Barrington-Hall. Lord Coulton. I have come to offer my very best wishes on your engagement.'

His blue eyes looked into hers, a shield across them today which allowed her nothing.

'Mr Moreland.' Her smile felt glued to her lips, but slipping.

He did not touch her, but kept his distance, a man merely giving his felicitations. A formal thing, prescribed and correct.

Barrett Brooker was next to him on one side and Lady Winifred Leggett on the other. Mr Brooker held an air of stiffness that she had not seen in him before, a sort of hesitation that made her wonder.

James took Mr Moreland's hand and shook it warmly. 'It is good to see you here, Oliver, and as you can probably tell I am more than delighted by my good luck.'

'You deserve each other because you are both good people.'

This was said with true sincerity, a note of something else underneath, and she felt the pain of his honesty inside her, the final truth of what would be.

Her notice went to the woman beside him and in that moment Esther simply let go of any tiny hope that she had not realised she had clung to.

What had she expected? Some given troth that might change everything? Some look that told her he wanted to take her hand and ask her to run away, together, into the future, leaving all of this behind them?

A nightmare.

A dream.

James's arm was warm beneath her fingers and Lady Leggett's smile was kind.

We are all exactly where we should be.

The phrase rang around in her head like the peal of bells in church.

Happiness was a measured thing, a thing of degree

and hope. There were no guarantees, of course, but laying down base stones helped: the traits one wanted in a marriage, the family surrounding a couple, the ease in which contentment could exist.

Contentment, but not love.

She swallowed down such words because the bitter truth in them shocked her.

Oliver watched Esther's hand tighten on the arm of Lord Coulton, her gloved fingers delicate and thin. As delicate as the rest of her, her smile a wan and pallid thing and nothing like the one he was more used to.

She was only just holding on, he thought next, and wondered how he could know that, but the tie that had always held them was still there, even in the face of her engagement, even with her would-be husband standing mere inches away from her.

Bringing Winifred with him as a buffer to this party suddenly looked like a foolish thing, her brittle perfection here jolting and aggravating. He wished she would not stand so close. He wished her hands did not lie upon his arm as if she owned him.

Esther looked soft and lost and alone in this room full of everyone she knew. He could see the child that he had discovered on that snowy street huddled in the doorway so long ago in her clearly. There was a darkness under her eyes and her mouth was tight.

Barrett had said she was happy. How could he even think that she was? Why did her family not see her sadness, her cousins, her uncle and her aunt?

Lord Coulton was the wrong husband for her even

with all his affability and his pleasantness. God, what would happen should her past resurface and a family like the Coultons, known for their puritanical beliefs, be faced with Alexandra's history?

All his former thinking of letting Esther go for her own good suddenly seemed like simply throwing her to the wolves. He would not be able to protect her.

Winifred chose that moment to lean across to him and whisper in his ear, 'Let us go from this place, Oliver. There is a warm bed at your apartment and plenty of wine.'

He could see that look in her eye that he usually warmed to, a wicked, impish teasing, and he knew that Esther would have seen it, too.

He needed to get away. He needed to be alone. Winifred was simply giving him an excuse to go.

He would give Barrett his goodbyes and then surely he could leave. He glanced at his timepiece. A good half an hour already was gone since his arrival. No one would expect more.

With a smile he tipped his head to the couple before him. 'I hope you will both be happy.'

Banal. Meaningless. But he no longer had the words he wanted to give to Esther and he could see her aunt across the room watching.

Lord Coulton's returning nod was enthusiastic. Esther barely acknowledged him and Winifred clung to him like a beautiful limpet as they crossed the crowded room to the door.

Outside he leant against the wall, drained of all energy.

Winifred looked concerned. 'Are you well?'

He shook his head. 'I think I might call it a night and go home. I can drop you off wherever you want.'

She turned, her eyes in the moonlight filled with tears. 'This is the end of us, isn't it?'

'Yes.' He could not lie. He could not say another thing that was not true.

'You have changed, Oliver. You have become… respectable.'

'I hope so,' he returned, and felt all the better for it.

Oliver Moreland was gone with the beautiful Lady Winifred Leggett. Gone home to bed, she imagined from the look on the woman's face and the whisper in his ear that held a quality that was unknown to her.

Sensuality, she thought, and there was a certain shocking exposure in the very word. She looked around at James and could not imagine such an emotion scrawled on his face.

What would it be like as a wife to go to bed with him? To wake up together every morning of her life from now until she was dead?

'What are you thinking, my dear?' James chose that moment to lean across and ask his question.

'That I am hungry and would like some supper,' she replied.

'Then let me escort you to the supper table and have our fill.'

Hours later Esther was finally able to find her own bed, though just as she had slipped between the sheets Charlotte appeared and jumped in beside her.

'Was that not a wonderful party, Esther? You looked beautiful and your husband-to-be is a good man.'

'He is indeed, and I am lucky.'

Charlotte frowned and turned towards her, tucking her bare feet under Esther's warmer legs.

'It's just what we always dreamed, isn't it? I asked you once what you were looking for in a husband and you replied you wanted a man who was kind, dependable and steadfast.'

'I did say that.'

'And I told you sometimes you should take a chance and be brave. Well, you have and look how happy you are, a girl about to be a wife within a wonderful family and with a man who is the heir to the riches of the Coultons and the title as well. No wonder Mama is so thrilled and cannot stop speaking of your choice to everybody she meets. And how lucky you did not say yes to the first man who caught your eye, too.'

'The first man?'

'Lord Alberton, of course, for you would have missed out then on Lord Coulton. The world is a strange place, is it not? One choice and you go this way, another choice and it is to somewhere else entirely.'

'Another life, you say?'

'Exactly.'

Apart from a whirl of society parties a week or so back, Oliver remained isolated and he knew that his balance was badly missing.

He could not quite bring himself to decamp to the loneliness of Elmsworth Manor because he felt off-kilter and a bit odd, but neither did he wish to venture back into society in the same way that he used to. He knew his mother had had these feelings, too, and he wondered if her condition could be an inherited one and if all the melancholy that had so influenced her life was now affecting his.

He'd gone back to drinking more than he should, knocking back the brandy in his late-night watches under the semi-darkness of his apartment.

Barrett was worried about him and so was Freddie, newly returned from Exeter and glowing with an inner light. He had found love with his flower heiress, it seemed, and Oliver did not have the heart in the face of such joy to lay his own problems down for discussion. So he stayed silent.

He never brought anyone home with him as he had once been wont to do and he shunned any public gathering where he knew Esther Barrington-Hall might be. Thus he avoided her, like the plague. He admitted this to himself as he downed the fourth glass of brandy in his library.

It was raining outside, hard, the weather one of constant wet greyness and the streets of London damp and sombre. The weather suited his mood. He had stopped exercising in Hyde Park just in case the Barrington-Hall party should be using it for their exercise and had not taken his horse out for nearly two weeks.

The only thing he had kept doing with any pleasure was visiting Whitechapel and making certain that things were in place for when he did fulfil his promise to his brother and move to Elmsworth Manor.

Winifred Leggett had called by several times, but he had managed to elude her and she had sent a terse and very angry note to him accusing him of distance. He had not bothered answering it. So when the door knocker rapped out loud and clear he tensed, waiting for his man to send whoever was there away, and was then surprised when he heard footsteps and voices coming towards him.

A quick knock and Julia stood at the door, removing her hat with a deft movement and coming to sit by the fire in the armchair opposite from him.

'I saw Barrett Brooker yesterday, Oliver, and he said you were holed up here and he could not budge you. As Phillip and Gretel have left for the Americas I thought what is left of our family ought to be checking that you are in good health.'

'I am.'

'You don't look it.'

He smiled. His aunt was always bluntly honest.

'When Miranda married your father I almost felt like I should warn him of my sister's long spells of despondence and sometimes in the years that followed I wished that I had.'

'Why?' Now this was a different conversation from the one he'd expected.

'Because your father, while a complex man, was also a good one. He tried hard to do his best, though

I know you could never quite see that. It was your mother who was the difficult half of their marriage.'

'I know.'

'You do?'

'Phillip left me his letters.'

'Parents have a lot to answer for when their children fail to understand them. It was why I never wanted children or marriage. I did not need the responsibility of shaping others when my family had been so poor at the job in the first place. It was not just Miranda who had problems. Our own parents were of the same mould.'

'But you escaped this melancholy?'

In light of what he had just been thinking, Oliver waited for her answer.

'Yes, and so did you. Phillip was not so lucky.'

'In what way?'

'He holds a sadness that he finds hard to control, but Gretel has helped him with that and he owes her much.'

'She is sick.'

'I know. She told me. That is why she wants to go to the Americas. Her parents are there and as she will need them at the end I think Phillip was glad to go.'

'The end of the line.' He said those words quietly, almost without thought.

'Not if you do something about it, it's not.'

'You mean marry and have children?'

'I do. Your mother, for all her faults, would have wanted you to move on with your life and so would your father.'

At that he laughed. 'My mother tried to kill me twice.'

'I wondered if you would have known that.'

'It was in the letters. You came to stay for a few months by all accounts to help her, but then she wanted you gone.'

'And I only left because I thought she was getting better.'

'And because you were sleeping with my father by that time?'

His aunt's face paled. 'I was and that is something I do not regret. He was sad and so was I. We clung to each other as if we were on a life raft in the middle of a raging sea.'

'And afterwards?'

'I moved back to London and seldom saw him.'

'He did not come to see you?'

'He did, but I made it plain that what we had done behind Miranda's back was wrong and I would not be a part of it any more if he stayed with her. After that he took to the bottle and never quite left it.'

'He loved you.' Suddenly it all made sense.

When his aunt burst into tears he knew that she had loved him back. After a moment or two she dabbed at her eyes with a handkerchief and sat up straighter.

'Life does not always turn out how you would want it to or indeed how you would expect it. Maybe if I had tried harder, fought for the chance...' She stopped. 'But I didn't.'

'Which is why you are here today?'

She smiled as she wiped her eyes. 'We always understood each other the best, Oliver, you and I. My guess is that the engagement of Esther Barrington-Hall has been hard for you.'

Hell. He did not want this. 'Your guess is the wrong one, Julia. I am merely tired, tired from the many injuries I have sustained lately and tired from rushing. I need to rest.'

'Can I give you one piece of advice?'

He nodded.

'Go to Elmsworth Manor and recover. It is the only place you will.'

'May I also ask you something, Julia?'

'Of course.'

'How did you stop loving my father?'

'I never did, but I wanted the best for him and he still needed to be helping Miranda for his own sanity. I told you he was a good man.'

'So in essence it was a protection that you gave him?'

This time she laughed. 'I had not thought of it before like that, but in a sense, yes, it was. One defends those one loves with all one's might.'

Lord Coulton had kissed her yesterday, in the garden of the Coulton town house under the sheltering privacy of the budding wisteria.

Her husband-to-be had asked her outside to talk, the weather for a change not so cold. She had put on a coat, just in case, and accompanied him, the lawn green with winter rain and the natural world full of promise.

'I want us to know each other better, Esther. I want

us to be the best of friends.' He stepped closer to her as he said this and she breathed in. 'In my family there is a rule that we all adhere to and that is if we are ever worried or unsure we talk about it. What do you think of such a directive?'

'It is a good one. I think my family is much the same.'

'You never talk of your own mother and father, though? What sort of people were they?'

She made herself stop for a moment before answering, 'My father liked his wine overmuch, unfortunately.'

'And your mother?'

'Tried to stop him drinking it, I suspect. Papa died when I was five, so I do not have many memories of that time.'

'And then you and your mother moved away?'

That sentence had her swallowing.

'Pardon?'

'Your aunt said that you moved away for a few years after your father died?'

'Oh, yes, we did. She had good friends to the north and so we went there. It was a lovely time for I do like the countryside, the greenness and the wide-open spaces where one is able to breathe.'

Such lies were horrible things, but they fell from her tongue slippery like silk because she was so adept at stretching the truth. Of all the things her mother had taught her, this was the one lesson that had truly stuck.

James looked pleased at her explanation and, when

a bird flew close to them with strands of straw in its beak, he changed the subject.

'The home we build will be a happy one, I am sure. I thought to relocate to Hertfordshire if this is something you might consider?'

'I would.' And she meant it. To be far from London, from memories, from all the things here that could harm her. From Oliver Moreland.

He kissed her then. He simply leant down and placed his mouth across her own so that she could feel his warmth and his closeness.

It was wet and the rasp of whiskers against her face stung. When his tongue invaded her mouth she stepped back.

'I am sorry,' he said. 'I thought…'

'I was surprised. I didn't know…'

'Of course you would not, for if I should make a guess I think that was probably your very first kiss?'

The flash of night came then, a laugh through the darkness and the fetid fumes of brandy. *Just a kiss, little girl. Just a kiss for your uncle and I will be happy.*

Shock claimed her with the unexpectedness of this memory, one she had had no true recollection of at all up until this second, but James was speaking again.

'Lovemaking is not a thing to be feared, Esther. No, it is a joy between two people who want to share and who want to know everything they can about each other.'

His hand cradled her face and this time when he kissed her it was softer, more tentative, a gentle kiss and one imbued with kindness.

'No need to rush, my love. We can get used to each other first and then it will be easier for you.'

When he let her go she stepped back, her hands fisted in the fabric of her coat, her heart beating loud and fast. She didn't want him to kiss her again, she didn't want the closeness. She didn't like his tongue in her mouth or his face pressed up against her own. And it wasn't because of the fact that she didn't know him. It was not because she was an innocent who had no experience with the sensual world of lovemaking, either.

Her mother on the bed tangled in the sheets, the musky smell of bodies around her, the noises, the sounds, the movements. The memories were all horrifying to her and dredged up again because of two kisses, given tentatively, carefully and with consideration by a man who would soon be her husband.

She did not want James Coulton to touch her again and she did not wish to touch him. She was the ruined daughter of a mother who had prostituted her body for drugs for years in the underbelly of London. There, it was said, not out loud but on the inside, the shards of truth digging into both pain and shame.

How would this ever work, this marriage? How could she be the wife that James wanted? One thing she did know was that she would never be truthful with him about her past, about her mother, about the lost degenerate years that had formed her into the person she now was. And in this admission she also forfeited any hope of change and of peace.

He took her hand even as she was thinking this and entwined his fingers into her own before bringing them up to his mouth and kissing the end of each finger in the gloves.

'We shall wait for the wedding to bed, my love, but before then there shall be plenty of opportunity to show you how wonderful a kiss can be, a caress, a hidden touch.'

He looked up at the house to make certain no one observed them and reached out to undo the button on her coat. Then his hand slipped beneath the heavy wool and cupped her right bosom over the thinner fabric in her gown.

'I do want you and you want me, too, and this is just another way we can find each other, Esther. A further path.'

He flicked her nipple and smiled. 'It hardens for me as your body calls for mine. Can you feel it? My God, I cannot wait to claim and own you.'

Even the words made her feel sick. Owning and claiming was what the men who had bedded her mother had mostly done, quickly, roughly and with little intention of staying.

The world began to spin and she fell against James, his hands catching her as he smiled.

'Ahh, you are so responsive. I cannot believe that I have been so lucky. But come, we must return to the house before I lose all caution.'

He re-buttoned her coat and took her hand, leading her inside with a wide smile upon his face.

She was sick that night, vomiting in her basin until her aunt called the doctor and it was decided she must spend the next two days in bed to shake off the malady that had downed her. No one was to visit save for her maid just in case the illness was a catching one.

The whole state of affairs pleased Esther as she lay there after they had all gone, a small candle flickering at her bedside and throwing quiet shadows all over the room.

She was cold and barren. She knew that she was and life after today would never be all right again. The sickness was inside her head and her heart and not even the most skilled physician in the land would be able to wheedle such a disorder from her. Damaged goods. Broken, spoiled and marred. A woman who was not fit to be anyone's bride.

She cried then quietly, the tears spilling down her cheeks and into the pillow, but she was careful not to make a sound.

'You look pale, Esther,' her aunt said when she came down for breakfast three mornings later, her first day of being downstairs again. 'I do hope you are not sickening for something else?'

'Perhaps she is just longing to be away from this house, Mama, and these questions.' Jeremy, who was also at the table, said this as he winked at Esther and dug into his own very large plate of bacon and eggs.

She was glad her cousin was there to divert the heart-to-heart talk she could see that her aunt was longing to have. After the kisses James had given her and her own reactions, she just could not face it.

'Did you hear Mr Moreland's brother, Phillip, has departed the country for America with his wife, Mama? I wonder if that means that Oliver Moreland will now take up residence at Elmsworth Manor. I must say that I can't see him too far from all his hedonistic pursuits in London.'

Esther made much of pouring herself a cup of tea as she listened to her cousin, not wanting to meet her aunt's eyes at all in such a discussion.

Elmsworth Manor. She wondered where it was exactly. She also wondered why the proper heir to the title would have left England to go so very far away. Another question in the dynamics of a family that posed many.

'Oliver Moreland would do well to leave and try to find some respectability. I know his aunt despairs of him ever finding a wife.'

'Well, it's not for his lack of options, Mama. He could propose to any female in England and she would say yes.'

'I doubt it, Jeremy. Mothers generally want someone for their daughter who is not so unrestrained.'

'Sometimes, Mother, I think you were born a century too late with your outdated ideas as to the wants and needs of the next generation.'

'Well, my son, you are to be twenty-four in two months. Women can be left on the shelf, but so, too, can young men, so be very careful for the choice soon begins to narrow.'

Her cousin laughed. '*Touché*, Mama.'

Aunt Mary had the grace to smile and the breakfast settled back down to an even keel, but all Esther could think about was the ruction in the Moreland family and what that might mean. Would Oliver Moreland leave for the Elmsworth estate? Would she ever see him again?

She swallowed a sip of tea and castigated herself roundly.

He is no longer anything to do with you, Esther. You cannot be acting this way every time you hear his name.

But she did keep thinking of him, without pause, all through her breakfast and into the day.

Chapter Nine

The whole family was at the Haversham ball five days later, the salons such a crush they could barely move through them.

Her aunt was scathing. 'This is just too crowded, Thomas, for let me tell you there is a fine balance between enough guests and far too many.'

Esther felt James by her side, his hand cupping her elbow and guiding her through after her family. She wished she was not here. The headache she had had for days and days was worse and her stomach was a tight bundle of knots.

The next salon was thankfully a little less crowded and though it was noisy she could now hear James's voice when he spoke.

'You look beautiful in green, Esther. The colour matches your eyes and I have missed seeing you across the past days. Did you get the flowers I sent?'

'Thank you, I did. The winter roses were a lovely pink.' Keep talking about nothing, she thought, for she did not want the more personal. She was scared of it. When Charlotte joined them Esther smiled at her.

'Sarah and Mr Brooker have just arrived. I saw them a moment ago and they said that they would come and find us. I don't think I have ever seen my sister look happier.'

A slight frown crossed her cousin's brow as she said this and Esther could imagine what she was thinking and made a better attempt at looking happy herself.

In this room she could see a good many of the Coultons, refined people who were probably wondering at the crowd present as much as her uncle and aunt were. Further afield stood the same man she had seen Oliver Moreland with that first time, a diminutive beauty beside him looking rather overawed by the whole affair.

For the hundredth time that night she prayed that he would not make an appearance.

A few hours later their party retired to the supper room and found drinks and food, the fare all beautifully presented and delicious.

The evening had not been as difficult as Esther might have imagined as, after dancing a few times with James, she had enjoyed the company of all her boy cousins and her uncle in other turns on the floor. James himself had been most circumspect, the man who had fondled her in the arbour a week ago tonight melded into a congenial society lord.

He was affable and considerate. He had danced

with Charlotte twice and with Aunt Mary once and her aunt had been flattered by his attention.

Two glasses of wine had also helped Esther relax, her worries dulling a bit and the glitter of the social occasion filling up the spaces left. She could learn to enjoy James's kisses, surely. They could practise and communicate and he had already said to her if there was a problem he wanted them to talk it over and solve it. That was a prudent and rational thing to say and he was a man who leant towards the reasonable.

Perhaps it would not be too hard to make the intimate more palatable. She just needed to loosen up around him and feel the way he respected her, loved her, needed her.

The next glass of wine helped again, and she smiled at him in the way of a woman who would be a wife and watched him smile back at her.

The shout came unexpectedly from a distance, a man's voice slurred by drink and harsh with anger.

'Alexandra? Is it you?'

She looked around and saw a large dark-haired man stride forward, incredulity on his face. The words did not register at first and she was as surprised as anyone else that someone should make such a fuss at a public ball.

'Alexandra? You're a whore and a prostitute. Why the hell would you be here?'

He advanced closer and then stood right before her, his mouth a sneer and his eyes furious.

'You are pretending to be a lady? My God, how

can you do that? You are nothing of the sort and you
know it. Get out. Get out.'

The last words came in an even angrier way and
for just a moment Esther thought he might lash out
and hit her, without a care in the world.

But he didn't. Rather, he stood there as puzzlement
crossed his brow, the horror of it all suddenly hitting
him. He swore and froze.

'Hell, you are the daughter? The little girl she had
with her in the brothels?'

Esther did not say a word. She just stood there with
her chin up, her heart beating fiercely and faced him
down until her uncle pushed himself between them
and took her arm, her aunt right behind them as they
led her out of the crowded room, past all the astonished expressions, a silence that was deafening following their every movement.

Lord Coulton did not follow.

Outside the carriage was sought, still no dialogue
between any of them.

Her uncle shouted at his driver to hurry in a rude
manner and in a tone she had never before heard
him use.

Charlotte came, too, and Sarah and the boys one
by one behind them.

A family united. A strong family who had her back
and had not deserted her, though she had an idea of
what such an action must have cost them.

This scandal would be all over London before the
hour was up and by morning everyone who was any-
body would know of it. They would know that her

mother had not been the gentle lady her aunt had purported she was, that it was no quiet holiday after all that they had taken to the countryside and that Esther's childhood had neither been idyllic nor suitable.

Ruination.

This was what it felt like, scurrying away on a wet night from the words of a drunken, angry and unpleasant stranger. This was what it sounded like, too, grounded in silence, the space between breaths.

When she and her aunt, uncle and girl cousins piled into the conveyance and closed the door to the world outside she felt relief.

'The boys will follow in the next carriage.' Aunt Mary's words were flat, furious and resigned.

There could be no coming back from this. They all knew it. There could be no refuting the accusations, either, because the truth had a certainty that was well recognisable.

Esther did not have the courage to look up as the coach hurtled through the deserted streets for home. She did not want to see what she knew would be in their eyes. Sorrow. Impotency. Shock.

Uncle Thomas would be desperately trying to work out a plan to go forward and Aunt Mary would be, too. Charlotte's hand crept into her own and squeezed and Sarah found a blanket to lay across their laps.

Warmth, friendship and a support that had never faltered once, not in all the years of her coming to them after the dreadful chaos with her mother.

Her aunt and uncle had known some of it, but now they, like everybody else in that room, knew it all.

She looked just like her mother, she had always known that, but she wasn't her mother and she would never make the same mistakes as Alexandra had, no matter what happened.

Uncle Thomas leant forward. He had refound his equanimity and his voice was soft. 'We will always be here for you, my dear, and our name is a powerful one. Powerful enough to protect you.'

She nodded and breathed out. She did not cry for she was beyond tears, the terror of her lost years wholly entwined in the voice of that man tonight. She would never escape it, never, and she could not drag a family of such honour through the mud again and again.

Her aunt had finally found her voice, too, and was full of a planned response. 'You will be married straight away, of course, in a ceremony that will protect you. Lord Coulton is a good man and he knows his allegiances are to you, the innocent party in all of this horror. Once you are married off and settled the scandal will pass as it always does, a whisper here and an unkind word there about your mother, but it will not intrinsically hurt you or your children. You will be safe, dear Esther, safe to go on with your life as you are meant to. The Coulton estate is far enough away from London to be a buffer and we will come and visit frequently. Society here does not need to see you for a while and you do not deserve to endure their censure.'

Her uncle was nodding. 'I shall speak to Coulton in the morning and explain things to him. You have a dowry, Esther, a generous one provided by us, so you are not penniless or without possibilities. You have been the veritable belle of the Season and a man like the one we have just encountered is a nobody. Did you hear his accent, Mary, for goodness' sake? He is from trade.'

Once home the life seemed to drain out from them all, the familiarity of their setting so different from this present and strange reality.

Uncle Thomas poured them all a brandy and made them drink it, the boys arriving home just as they had begun.

'I should have slugged him.' Ben's voice held nothing but anger.

'We can go back and find him after we see Esther is all right and then we can give him all he deserves.' Aiden made this comment.

'I know his name. He won't escape this slander, by God he will not.' Jeremy, normally the most equable of all her cousins, looked ready to leave this very moment.

'No.' Her uncle's voice. 'We will wait till the morrow when our tempers have cooled and then we will sort this out.'

All of them looked at her.

'I don't want anyone hurt.'

Benjamin laughed but it was not a happy sound. 'Too late for that, Esther. We have been already.'

The collective 'we' was reassuring and she took in a breath to state that which she did not want to.

'Everything he said was true. Mama was a prostitute who was addicted to strong drugs and would do
anything to get them. Anything.'

'God.' Charlotte swore now and no one corrected
her, not even Aunt Mary.

'It was not your fault,' Sarah said, just as Esther
knew she would. Clever, analytical Sarah with a mind
that was logical and lucid. 'Your mother was never
happy with my uncle. Our grandmother told me that.
She was damaged, somehow, and could never find all
her pieces and stick them back together. But you can,
Esther. You can find your life in all of this and live it,
well and happily and away from society just as Mama
said. You might even be happier out of London, for
I know I will be. Barrett and I do not plan to stay in
the city, either, so we can see you and James as much
as our hearts desire it, which shall be all of the time.'

A different road, and the way that Sarah laid it out
a road that would not be hard to travel. Perhaps in this
she could find a resolution, a way to go forward that
was not impossible.

Her aunt did not look totally convinced and Esther
suddenly worked out why. The one part of the puzzle
that was necessary to make this all happen was missing: Lord Coulton.

She wondered why he had not followed her here
to the family home in St James's Square to give them
his own take on this turn of events.

She had started the evening with the hope that her
husband-to-be would remain distant and ended it hoping he would be close.

* * *

An hour later when the clock struck the hour of three she knew he would not come, they all did, the unspoken dread in the room cloying and sickening.

Her happy ending depended on her groom-to-be and, if he absconded, she doubted that there would be another to fill his place.

Esther rose late, the sleepless night taking its toll. She had a sore stomach and her eyes were puffy from crying.

She dressed carefully, though, because much could be made of appearances and because she did not wish her family to realise that she was as flattened as she felt.

Her maid helped dress her hair and applied a small puff of perfume to each wrist. 'For courage,' she said quietly and Esther understood that both upstairs and downstairs her ruin would have been spoken of.

'Thank you.'

Would James arrive this morning? Would he rush in on a white horse and sweep her off to the future? Such nonsense made her smile and, given that yesterday morning that was the last thing she would have wanted, none of it made any sense.

Another of the servants came with a message stating that her uncle would like to see her in the library when she was ready to come down.

Looking at the clock in the upstairs passageway, she was surprised to see it was nearly two in the afternoon.

Her aunt and uncle were waiting for her and as the servant announced her they stood. Almost in fright.

'How are you today, my dear? I hope you had some sleep?'

'Some,' she answered, thinking as she looked at them how tired they both appeared.

Showing her to a chair, Uncle Thomas waited till they all sat. Placing his elbows on his knees, he then leant forward and took in a breath.

'I am very sorry to tell you this, Esther, but Lord Coulton has withdrawn his suit for your hand in marriage. He states that he no longer wishes to be your husband.'

'I see.'

'He is a cad and a bounder and I never expected it of him, but…well…that is what we are left with.'

'And good riddance, I say.' Her aunt chirped in with this, though her uncle spoke again as she finished.

'The Coulton family is citing untruthfulness and incompatibility. I myself call their reactions a complete lack of courage and one which shows poor moral fibre.' He stopped for a moment before going on. 'The thing is, his defection has led to a sort of domino effect and the list that I gave you with twenty suitable young men on it has now dwindled down to none.'

'It is incomprehensible,' her aunt said before tailing off as her husband raised his hand.

'Your aunt and I realise that this has put you in a difficult position, Esther, but there is no cause to make a quick decision of where we go from here until we see the proper lay of the land. We thought to relocate and simply go back home to Kent. Six months should do it.'

'What of Sarah's wedding? What of the Season for Charlotte?'

'I think we all know the answer to those questions. We need to be out of society and away from its censure until we can return on another tack.'

'Like a ship?' She asked that question in nervousness.

'Indeed, and one that has sailed through a terrible storm,' her aunt went on. 'One that is ragged and broken and dreadfully hurt, but one that in finer weather can once again find its strength and sail in calmer waters.'

'I see.' And she did. They were willing to sacrifice themselves along with her no matter how dreadful the accusations. The defection of Lord Coulton and all of the suitors did not extend to them.

'Thank you for helping me.'

'You are welcome, my love, and remember family will never desert you.'

Like her mother had?

'Perhaps now after all this commotion you would enjoy playing a hand of whist with me in the drawing room, Esther, to help us both relax.'

She smiled at her aunt's suggestion, but shook her head. 'Actually, I think I will return to bed and try to catch up on a few of the hours of sleep that I missed out on last night.'

She knew she wouldn't, of course, but she needed some time to make sense of what had just happened, to see a way for herself into the future.

* * *

Barrett Brooker arrived at Elmsworth Manor just after ten o'clock at night from London, the time frame telling Oliver that something was very wrong.

'You need to sit down to hear this,' Barrett said as they repaired to the library. 'Where is a bottle of your finest brandy while we are at it?'

'I hope you are not about to tell me that you are going to renege on your promise to marry Miss Sarah Barrington-Hall for I think that would be a great mistake.'

'A good guess, Oliver, and one that runs somewhat along the lines of what I am going to tell you next.'

'Miss Barrington-Hall has said she will not marry you? She has changed her mind?'

Barrett shook his head and began to speak.

'Two nights ago in the crowded ballroom of the Havershams a man stepped out of the crowd and proclaimed in the loudest of voices that Miss Esther Barrington-Hall's mother, Alexandra, was a prostitute and a whore and one who had plied her trade for years in the seething underbelly of an amoral London, her small daughter in tow.'

Shock hit him in a single unmitigated blow.

'Damn him to hell. What happened then?'

'The Barrington-Halls left the venue immediately, *en famille*, I might add, and with the grace that is so much a part of them, a solid and unified front of respectability shielding their niece with all they were worth. The place exploded into conjecture after they had gone as others who had heard put in their two pennies' worth until there was no stopping the gossip and the ugly blather that followed. Coulton departed almost as immediately with his entire family and I thought, well at least the man had gumption and was about to do the right thing.'

'But he didn't?' Oliver knew what was coming next.

'Yesterday morning he withdrew from their engagement citing family differences, undisputable falsehoods and the disappointment of being taken as a gullible fool by a family who should have known better.'

'He did not mince his words, then.'

'He did not. The point is, from there on every other suitor who had put their name forward to be considered by Miss Esther Barrington-Hall also withdrew their name until there was no one left. I have this on the good authority of my bride-to-be, you understand, so there can be no miscommunication. Esther Barrington-Hall is ruined. I doubt she will ever receive an offer of marriage again.'

Barrett finished his glass and helped himself to another one and Oliver watched him with a fire of fury inside.

'Where is Esther now?'

'At St James's Square. Sarah says she is talking of leaving London altogether with the dowry provided for her.'

'To do what?'

'No one is sure. Everybody is trying to find a solution. Personally, I think Thomas Barrington-Hall would like to marry her off to the next man who might step forward and that would be a huge mistake.'

'Why?'

'Because Sarah implied that Esther is broken by this, shattered into so many little pieces that she does not know how to put them together again.'

'What else does she say?'

'She says that the perfect life Esther had imagined for herself is now gone and her unrequited love for Coulton is not something to be got over easily. Sarah has heard her crying deep into every night since, but Esther will not talk much about it to anyone at all. Charlotte is at her wits' end and Lord and Lady Duggan are livid.'

'At her?'

'At Coulton. The boys want to hang, draw and quarter him, but Thomas Barrington-Hall says that if anyone touches the man it will be him.'

Oliver stood, going over to the window that overlooked the lake, seeing himself there reflected in the glass.

Choices in life were sometimes easy and sometimes hard. His mother had made the wrong choice and his father had tried in his way to make the right one. Esther had had a difficult childhood, but had been saved by the Barrington-Halls. But now she was broken again and in need of rescue. He had done it before and he could again, but this time he would do it in a different way.

'I will leave before light early tomorrow morning for London, Barrett, and you are welcome to join me for the ride. I shall take the four-horse conveyance so it should be a quick journey and we won't be stopping anywhere.'

At half past eleven in the morning her aunt came up the stairs and knocked at her door.

'Please make yourself tidy, Esther, and come down to the blue salon. There is something important we need to talk to you about.'

Dread filled her. Had Lord Coulton changed his mind? Was she to be asked to throw herself before him and beg for his forgiveness despite all the terrible things he had said? Or had other rumours surfaced, worse ones, ones that outlined the way her mother had died, by her own hand?

'Is there some sort of a problem?' she said, but her aunt stopped her with a single shake of her head, an air about her that was different from the past few days.

Esther pushed down the fabric in her simple dark blue gown, trying to lessen the creases, and followed Aunt Mary down the stairs.

To one side a maid gazed at her, her eyes full of tears, and she looked away.

Pity had a certain flavour that she had never liked and while her secrets had escaped their tightly locked box, none of what had happened had been her fault. None of it. She repeated the phrase as she came into the formal blue salon with her chin up.

To almost fall down with astonishment. Mr Oliver Moreland stood there with her uncle, dressed in his very best clothes, his hair combed back, hat in hand as if one of the servants in their surprise had forgotten to take it from him and hang it on the pegs just inside the front door.

He looked stately, noble and magnificent. And he looked as though he meant business.

'Miss Barrington-Hall.' His dark blue eyes took in her own and told her nothing.

'M-Mr Moreland.' She could barely say his name.

'It is good to see you again.' More words that told her nothing. The clock in the corner showed eighteen minutes to twelve in the morning and outside the sky held patches of blue. Time and life went on in surprising ways and this development was the most surprising of them all.

Uncle Thomas then began to speak. 'Mr Moreland has heard of your dilemma, Esther. He has heard of Lord Coulton's betrayal and of your many other suitors who have simply evaporated into thin air.'

She glanced at Oliver Moreland, who did not look pleased at her uncle's explanation. She could see a muscle in his jaw working as he bit down on a reply.

'So he has come to offer a solution to us all, for he realises that ruination is upon you, fairly and squarely, and there can be no going forward for you unless—'

Their visitor broke in over her uncle's words. He looked impatient and irascible. 'Your uncle is trying to explain that I have come to offer you my hand in marriage, Miss Barrington-Hall, if you will have it.'

Of all the things that he might have said, this was

the least expected and for a moment she could not quite place his meaning.

'You are…asking me…to marry you?'

'I am.'

'Why?'

Even in company she could not help but ask for his reasons.

Her uncle jumped in. 'You will never get another offer as good as this one, Esther, for Mr Moreland is proposing the perfect solution to a predicament that has haunted us for all these days. Without this tender I am uncertain as to how you will ever find a future again for it is a gift from above and you should be eminently grateful. I know your aunt and I both are.'

There was no talk of love or even of liking.

Oliver Moreland looked hard and stern and angry, and Esther wondered what he was getting from this bargain given it was weighted so heavily in her favour. He hardly appeared like a suitor desperate to win her hand with flowery words and grand gestures. No, he looked like a wealthy man who was in a place he did not want to be, asking a woman to marry him whom he barely knew.

'I do not think…' she said and stopped, swallowing as she tried to rearrange her thoughts. He would never be happy with her, not in a million years, with her past around her neck like a millstone. Her own private reaction to Lord Coulton's intimacy was another problem altogether.

'May I have a few moments alone with your niece, Lord Duggan?'

This came from Oliver Moreland and relief crossed Uncle Thomas's face as he consented and pulled her aunt from the room.

Then they were alone, the silence broken only by the chirp of a bird outside the window, hopping from bare branch to bare branch on the cherry tree.

'I realise, of course, that we hardly know each other, Miss Barrington-Hall, and you have just been hurt to the core by a man you loved and trusted and one who should have acted in a far better manner.'

His eyes held hers questioningly when she blinked, trying to find an equilibrium.

'Lord Coulton is a bastard.'

The strong language made her flinch.

'And you, believe it or not, have just had a damned lucky escape.'

More swearing.

'We are strangers, but I feel we could deal well together. I would not expect anything you did not wish to give me. That I promise you, Esther.'

Her name. Soft. Like a whisper.

'The wedding itself will have to be simply and quickly done so that we can escape London and go to Elmsworth Manor, my family estate. The isolation is probably just what you need right now. A place to heal and become strong again. And then, perhaps…'

He did not finish and she did not ask what he meant by it.

He was pulling a wide ring from his finger now, gaudy gold with an engraving across it, a prominent ruby at its centre. Stepping nearer to her, he held the bauble out, being careful all the time not to touch.

'Will you marry me?'

She nodded because she could not say otherwise and because she knew he was her very last chance of redemption. But was she saying yes to a flawed union with little chance of survival and the propensity to destroy her entirely when it fell to bits or could there be a chance of happiness for them?

He pushed the ring into the palm of her hand just as her aunt and uncle trudged back into the room, Aunt Mary catching sight of his offering and audibly gasping.

My God, that was badly done, he thought, his proposal sandwiched between the few minutes of privacy the Duggans had allowed him and a woman who looked as though she wanted nothing at all to do with any betrothal ever again.

Esther appeared beaten with the dark circles under her eyes and her nose reddened from high emotion. She looker thinner, too, and sadder and less sure, the girl out on the balcony at the Creighton ball diminished here and frightened. Every nail on the hand holding his ring was bitten down to the quick.

She had not put the ring on, either, but held it there as though unsure as to what to do, shades of the carriage all those years ago coming back in force. He should have brought one of his mother's or grandmother's rings with him from the treasure trove of jewellery at Elmsworth. He should have placed it on her finger, too, with care, but she had looked as though she did not wish for him to touch her, her hand shaking and her eyes bruised with caution.

In all truth he did not quite know what he was doing here, rushing from Elmsworth Manor as he had and proposing to Esther Barrington-Hall like his very life depended upon it.

My God, he knew her only fleetingly, the tie from their past doing things to him that he could not understand and her beauty finishing him off. All shallow things in the light of day in the blue salon of the Duggans' town house in St James's Square. But there it was.

Every encounter with Esther had ended with him castigating himself over some deficit perceived and such a reaction worried him because before meeting her he'd seldom let anyone rattle him.

Lady Duggan was looking at him in a way that also made him uncomfortable, her more usual wary censure replaced by sheer and utter gratitude. Being the answer to someone's prayers was not an easy place to be in.

'The ring is lovely, Esther, and with this proposal you can re-enter society with your head held high. Mr Moreland's name will give you back dignity and respect. It is a miracle.'

A week ago that would have been the very last thing she might have said, but expedience was a thing that could be twisted when circumstances demanded and every mother in the *ton* with an unmarried daughter knew that.

Lord Duggan on his behalf hurried across to an

impressive cabinet on one side of the room and poured four long fluted glasses with what he presumed to be wine. The older man handed one to each of them.

'To new beginnings, as unexpected as they are.'

Oliver raised his glass and took a few large gulps for he badly needed some sort of fortification. Esther took a tiny sip only.

The aunt and uncle clinked theirs together, trying to be jolly for the purpose of simply getting through this moment.

He could not reassure them because he did not know the rules of this game that he had begun. There was no light banter of acknowledging how perfect they were for each other or how they had known from the first that they were meant to be together. No shy smiles or sexual tension.

There was only tension on the Duggans' faces, puzzlement on his own and agony on Esther's.

'I want us to be married today. I have already procured a special licence and the minister from my parish in Hampshire is waiting in the carriage in order to provide his services.'

'Now?'

Esther said this as a whisper and looked around, as if she expected Oliver Moreland's parson to simply charge through the door. Her hands fell to the skirt of the dress she wore, the fabric plain and dark blue.

Not a wedding dress. Not a wedding day, not a wedding groom who was patient and gentle and understanding.

Oliver knew that if he did not marry her here and

now, something would take her from him, a better argument or the voice of reason, he knew not which, but the licence burned in his pocket and the hands on the clock in the corner of the room were turning.

Once it was done he could deal with everything else and away from the sharp gaze of the Duggans. Esther might manage to understand that while he was not an optimum choice his hand in marriage was none the less better than any of the alternatives.

An old maid. A governess. A woman who would live all of her life in the home of her guardians, attending to their needs as society shunned her.

When she looked at him it was almost as if she could read his mind, for the frown across her green eyes had sharpened and her bottom lip trembled.

God, please do not make her cry. Anything but that. Let her weigh up her options in a logical, measured way and understand that he was not the worst of them, after all.

He finished his drink and put the glass down, refusing more because he needed all of his wits today.

'May I ask Mr Curtis, the minister, in?'

Lady Duggan swallowed and nodded, not even trusting herself to speak. Lord Duggan looked flattened, the events of the past days no doubt exhausting.

'I think it would be for the best, my dear,' he said to Esther, who did not even attempt an answer. 'The protection of Holy Matrimony shall stop the gossip like nothing else could. Even if it is hastily done.'

He stooped and rang a small bell sitting on the

table and the same servant Oliver had seen at the door came in.

'There is a man in the Elmsworth carriage outside, Bertram, by the name of Mr Curtis. Could you please go and get him and ask him to come in?'

'Certainly, sir.' He shut the door firmly after him. To keep the rest of the Barrington-Halls out, Oliver surmised. He was certain Lady Duggan would have ordered that.

He tried to smile at Esther, but his lips were dry and she only looked away. His finger felt bare without the ruby ring of his grandfather's that he had worn constantly and for years.

Oliver Moreland did not wish to be here. He was tense and angry and distant. He might even be drunk, she thought, as he smiled at her, his mouth crooked and his eyes hard.

The ring in her hand was weighty. An expensive piece, no doubt, and plainly unsuitable. He had come to ask for her hand in marriage and had not even thought to bring a ring, dragging this piece off his own finger so that the gold was still warm.

If she had been braver, she might have simply said *No, I shall not marry you* and left it at that, but ruination was an alarming thing and the years to come of dreadful alternatives kept her silent.

The door opened and Bertram was there again, this time with a tall, thin man in tow, the raised collar at his neck proclaiming his vocation to the world.

'I am pleased to be at your service,' he said, and his

voice was soft and pleasant. Then he waited, hands before him threaded in a gesture of quietness.

Oliver Moreland pulled a document from the pocket of his jacket and the man looked over it.

'Everything appears to be in order, sir.' His eyes met Esther's. 'Miss Barrington-Hall, I presume.'

She nodded.

'Lord and Lady Duggan will act as our witnesses.'

Mr Moreland's voice again, formal and short, as if he wanted this to be finished as quickly as it possibly could be, without argument or fuss.

A moment later they were standing before Mr Curtis.

No flowers. No music. No wedding dress. No cousins.

A wedding as ruined as the bride was.

'For what is wedlock forced but a hell?'

The words her mother had often said when she was sad or drunk. How many times had she heard Alexandra say this and now she was living it?

'We are gathered together here in the sight of God, and in the face of this congregation.' Mr Curtis stalled and looked around, a pastor out of tune with what was happening.

A few small coughs and he began again.

'In the sight of God to join together this Man and Woman in Holy Matrimony...'

Oliver Moreland made no show of recognising his pastor's mistake, though her aunt next to her looked up quickly.

Her wedding. It was nothing at all like the one she

had imagined lying in bed with Charlotte and Sarah across the last years, each embellishing their own version of the most important day of their lives.

She said her lines in a trance and listened to her groom's replies. And then it was over, the rain on the windows, the ring on her finger, the document signed with a pen and some ink her uncle had retrieved from the writing desk by the door.

Oliver Benedict Arthur Moreland.

His writing was neat and he wrote with his left hand. All the many things she did not know about him counterbalanced against the very few that she did.

An hour later Esther was packing a large case of things that could be taken in the Elmsworth carriage to Elmsworth Manor. Her aunt sat on her bed and watched.

'I will see that all your other belongings are carefully transported across to Hampshire, my love. The gowns you picked out before have been wrapped in calico and taken by a maid to the conveyance already, for Mr Moreland said there would be some room for them.'

'Thank you.' Her voice sounded strange even to her own ears.

'May I also give you some advice, Esther?'

'Of course.' She stopped folding one of her jackets and looked over at her aunt.

'Love comes in many forms. You may have imagined Lord Coulton was the only one for you, but…' She stopped and reached over to take Esther's hand.

'Your mother had loved another man before she married your father and she made the mistake of hankering for him even after the wedding, even after knowing that such a union could never be.' She cleared her throat and began again. 'When one partner loves a lot and the other hardly at all it is a recipe for disaster, so at least with Mr Moreland you have the propensity to build your relationship from a place of equality. My advice would be to get to know him and let him know you, and then who can predict what might follow?'

'Who was the man she loved? My mother?' This was so unexpected, this small piece of information that explained a lot about her mother's wildness.

'Your father's best friend, Lord Spencer Henley. He died in an accident a few months before Alexandra married your father and she never quite recovered from that loss. Thomas and I thought your parents' relationship doomed, but Alexandra became pregnant with you and so...'

'You hoped it would be a new beginning?'

'Nothing is ever certain in any marriage, Esther, and you have to work through the hard moments to get to the good ones. Your mother did not wish to do that. She simply let your father go without even trying, although his drinking was certainly a big factor in that decision, so I admit it was not all one sided.'

Her aunt's fingers toyed with the far too big ruby ring on the fourth finger of her niece's left hand.

'What does not fit at the beginning can change

if you make an effort. Will you promise me to re-member that?'

Esther nodded.

'You are a good girl, Esther, a sensible and level-headed girl, a girl who will know that what you have been offered by Mr Moreland is a chance at becom-ing all the things your mother never allowed herself to be. Your uncle and I shall journey to Hampshire to see you in a month, which should give you the time to meld and grow together. If, however, you need us at any point beforehand you just need to send a let-ter and we will come. You know that, don't you? We are not abandoning you, not by any means, but we do think this union is for the best.'

'I know.'

'Good. Now let us finish the packing and then go and say goodbye to your cousins. They will, of course, be full of questions, but do not worry, for I shall attempt to answer all of them when you have gone.'

Chapter Ten

Mr Curtis sat across from them, a Bible on his lap.

Esther looked out of the window, at the fields and the hills. A beautiful open countryside and one she had never seen before.

Oliver Moreland spoke to his man of affairs of his estate, the parishioners who were in need and the ones who were in trouble.

Listening, she thought he knew a lot about them, this son of an extensive manor, another chatelain of a holding that had been in his family all down through the years.

It was a surprising side of him.

'We will stop at the Three Lions' Inn to water the horses and for a bite to eat. It lies about an hour and a half away, so if you wish to close your eyes you would have the time.'

She blushed at his care and thanked him as he found a blanket and held it out to her. When she swiped her hair back from her cheek in nervousness, she saw his glance go to the ruby ring.

'It was my grandfather's.' He said this quietly. 'But I shall find you another more suitable one on our return to Elmsworth.' Esther saw the fingers on his left hand go to the third finger of his right one as if in habit and wondered. Perhaps the ruby ring was something he had always worn? Perhaps it had sentimental value? The gaudiness in it dulled a little and she curled her fingers in towards her palm, keeping it in place.

Alexandra had sold every piece of jewellery she'd owned until there was nothing left. She had even taken the silver bracelet Esther had received on her fifth birthday from Aunt Mary and Uncle Thomas and pawned it for more of the white powder that allowed her the dream world she was happiest in.

What would her mother have made of today, she thought, wed to the man who had helped them at one of their lowest points and journeying now to a country estate as his bride?

Mr Curtis was watching her closely, though as she smiled at him he tipped his head and looked away and silence fell inside the carriage.

She came awake as the horses slowed, her head fallen against Mr Moreland's shoulder in her slumber. She immediately sat up.

Her hat was set now at a strange angle across her face and she readjusted it, glad for something to do.

If he noticed he made no show of it, merely observing the façade of the inn they were pulling up to in interest.

'It's been a while since I stopped here,' he said to no one in particular, though Mr Curtis took up the implied question.

'It is very good, sir. The new owners have put their heart and soul into the place to make it the best inn to sup at for miles.'

After helping her down the steps of their conveyance Oliver Moreland moved slightly away and Mr Curtis did not join them as they mounted the front steps.

They were then shown to a room at the front of the main downstairs parlour, a fire burning bright and a table set for two with good silver cutlery and napkins.

'Mr Curtis won't be eating with us?'

'No, he will seek his own repose in the bar, I expect.'

Esther was surprised. 'An unusual place for a man of the cloth to inhabit?'

'He has rheumatism and the ale helps him with that. He also knows the barman well.'

'From travelling often up and down these roads?'

'No. The man is his brother.'

'Disparate professions, then?'

He laughed and she liked the sound of it.

For the first time since asking her to marry him his bride felt familiar, the same woman for whom he had rushed into a flower seller in Covent Garden and procured his ridiculous bouquet of green sage and white roses.

She looked a bit happier, too, the pale of her cheeks

more flushed here, though that could be a result of the substantial flames in the fireplace beside them or of the wine they were sharing.

'Is Elmsworth Manor far from here?'

'Another hour, at least.'

He could see she wanted to ask other questions of the place so tried to tell her something of it.

'My older brother, Phillip, usually lives there, but he has gone on a trip to the Americas with his wife. As a second son I have made my life elsewhere, with other interests and business ventures.'

'But you were brought up at Elmsworth Manor?'

'I was, but I left when I was ten for boarding school and never fully resided in it again.' He took a drink of his wine and leant back. 'I knew this land well once, though, as Phillip and I rode across it from one edge to the other.' He pointed to a river in the far distance. 'My brother and I would fish there often and bring home the catch. The cook would then dress it up for dinner and congratulate us as the feast was served.'

'You were close, then, as brothers?'

He smiled, but did not seem inclined to follow through with this topic. 'Where was it you were raised before your mother took you away?'

'In Kent at the estate of the Duggans, for my father had his own accommodation separate from the main house. After Papa died Mama and I left.'

'For London?

She nodded.

'That must have been a hard place to be alone in without an extended family?'

'You saw Alexandra when she was at her worst, sir.' Esther heard the hitch of sadness in her voice. 'There were some good times, too, but I was young and had no real way of making her happy.'

'It was not your fault. Your mother made her own choices.'

'I know.' Squeezing the material in the table napkin together, she felt tense.

'If you ever want to talk about it?'

'I don't. After the last few days…' She stopped, finding no words for all the distance she felt.

'You need another topic? A happier one.'

Her eyes were even more beautiful than he remembered them and for a moment he toyed with the idea of saying so. But she would not want to hear that from him and so he refrained. They needed to get to know each other, to understand what drew them together and all the things that held them apart.

So instead he spoke of the weather and of Hampshire, bland and ordinary things, even as his ruby ring blinked on her marriage finger in the light of the candles from above.

He remembered his beloved grandfather giving him the ring as a young boy and telling him it had secret properties that would allow its wearer great safety. Perhaps even then his grandfather had seen the madness in his mother and had been worried by it. Oliver had seldom taken it off since manhood and though of late he had had a number of close encounters with death, he had recovered. He hoped it would protect Esther, from worry and from sadness and all the other hurts he could so often see in her.

They arrived at Elmsworth Manor in the late afternoon just before dusk, an orange light across the house that made it look like an estate from past times, the lines of it steep and crenulated, pale stone reflecting the sunset.

It sat on a hill with wide lawns undulating down to a lake, its black depths seen as they came along a drive edged in tall oaks, the branches bare at this time of the year, the buds still dormant in their hard brown casings.

'It is beautiful,' Esther said with feeling.

'My brother, Phillip, will be back to claim it when he is ready.'

He did not say this in any way that made her think he was bitter or sad. He said it with a gladness, rather, as if he did not wish to be burdened with such a reminder of family when according to all she had heard, his own had been so very difficult. She wondered then where he would live, where they would live, but did not feel she had the right to ask him of it.

Everything today made her feel exhausted and yet underneath the weariness a small excitement crept. No one would find her here. She was far from London and far from the *ton*, who liked nothing better than to gossip. She missed her family, but she would see them in a month when they ventured across to Hampshire to find out how she fared.

A month to try to find her place here. She did not

dare to hope that love between her and Oliver Moreland might blossom but she wanted them to be friends. A civil union. Unlike the marriage of her mother's.

Mr Curtis had spent the last hour asleep, but he woke now and prepared himself for the arrival. He had not said much for a man of the cloth, which was unusual because all the church men she had met had been far more verbose. Yet he seemed a kind man.

As the carriage pulled up at the front of the house and stopped, Esther felt herself caught between lives. Her day had lurched from shock to surprise to wonder and she had a headache because of it. In truth, all she wanted to do was lay her head down on a soft pillow in the darkness, a silence all around her, where she could take in her change of circumstances and make some sense of it.

Esther was wilting visibly in front of him and when Mrs King came to greet them at the front door he asked the housekeeper to take his new bride upstairs to the Rose Room.

'My wife has a headache,' he said by way of explanation and saw astonishment at the title mark the woman's face before she could hide it. Tomorrow would be soon enough to inform the staff properly of his marriage, but right now he wanted Esther cared for in the very best of ways. 'Could you make sure to provide a tray with light food and drink before she sleeps?'

'Certainly, sir,' Mrs King replied, gesturing the way

to Esther and leading her upstairs. She did not look back at all as she left.

Doffing his coat, Oliver walked into the library, the only room in the house that felt at least partly like his own, and after pouring himself a drink he sat behind the desk and took a sip.

'To marriage,' he whispered under his breath. The differences and flaws between himself and Esther could bring them together or destroy even the little communion that they had and right at this moment he had no true idea as to which direction it would go.

But Esther was safe with him at least, tucked into a soft bed in the Rose Room, her reputation, if not entirely reinstated, at least not gone altogether. She might be sad, lonely and hurting, but marriage was something he would not give up on and one day she would know that.

It would have to be enough.

He bent to the bottom drawer and retrieved the book with the yellow ribbons that Phillip had given him.

Of all the voices of his family, it was his father's that came out the strongest and the clearest from the letters and documents within.

There were a number of pages devoted to the sums of money left to the school Oliver attended in order to placate the headmaster when he was about to be thrown out for one or another misdemeanour. The many avenues the Earl had explored to try to find help for his wife with her continued sadness was also another thick file, but it was his father's diary entries that were the

most illuminating. These had been written fairly constantly over the years before his mother's death and
contained notes on the worry he felt for his sons and
their future and the wearying constant supervision for
a wife who seemed hell-bent on killing herself.

That, of course, led to the worst information in the
whole book, but he shut the covers firmly and refused
to think about it again tonight.

Phillip and he were lucky to survive their childhood, that much was plain. Now he just had to survive this marriage.

Esther lay and watched shadows from the branches
outside the windows send moonlight in dancing
movements on to the ceiling above.

The maid had pulled the curtains when she had
helped her into bed, but Esther had got up to throw
them wide open as soon as she left so that the vista
before Elmsworth Manor might be seen. The tray of
food and drink had arrived and she picked up a few
of the tasty titbits.

Where was Oliver Moreland's room?

She was very still as she listened for movements
in the passageway outside, but none came, the silence
of the place complete.

This was her first night in years away from her
family and anxiety began to gather. What were Charlotte and Sarah doing now? They had been shocked
at the news she'd been married so quickly and her
husband's distant demeanour hadn't calmed their
worries at all.

Charlotte had found paper and pen and stuffed it into a small cloth bag, gold coins in a purse added to the bottom.

'This is if you have to reach us, Esther. Write a note and send it and we will come. I promise.'

Sarah had been less dramatic.

'Mr Moreland is Barrett's best friend, Charlotte, so I hardly think he will put Esther in a garret and feed her crusts.'

'There are other ways a bride can be lonely, Sarah,' her youngest cousin had returned solemnly and Esther was rather alarmed to see Sarah nod her head at that.

Other ways? Sexual ways?

She turned her head over into the pillow and held her breath for a moment.

Her mother had used sex as a weapon to get exactly what she wanted and as a result Esther's own attitude towards the intimate was distorted.

Lord Coulton's kiss came back, the horror multiplied with memory. What if Oliver Moreland wanted to kiss her? Would she feel the same? Would he want intimate relations tomorrow night after he felt her enough rested? Or tomorrow morning? Would he come here tonight to her room after instructing the servants to stay away? Every rumour she had ever heard of him pointed to a man who enjoyed the sensual. Why should that simply stop now that he was married?

It wouldn't.

Yet perhaps she might like Oliver Moreland's

kisses a lot better than she had liked Lord Coulton's, for even the thought of them seemed preferable.

The door was locked. She had turned the key and checked to see that it did not budge. A safe place for now. Tears began to fall, huge fat tears that were a product of a difficult week. She did not make a sound, though, as she cried, just in case someone was stationed outside her room listening, her fingers tightly held against her mouth.

When she felt calmer she pondered again on the fact that she had enjoyed the touch of her new husband's hand at the balls and she had liked his closeness in the dancing. Perhaps it would be all right? Perhaps with the correct person bodies knew how they were supposed to react?

Everything was askew. Sarah had entered into her betrothal with love, but Esther did not exactly know what emotions sat around her own.

Relief. Gratitude. Hope. Despair. A whole range of feelings and ones that she had no way of knowing which might triumph.

Chapter Eleven

Oliver met Esther the next morning in the dining room. He stood as he saw her approach, gesturing her to a seat opposite, a large breakfast set out on the table before him. She looked beautiful in a natural way, uncluttered by all the makeup and flashy items he more usually saw on women. Her gown was of gold velvet, plainly cut but well tailored, showing off the shape of her body.

'I hope you slept well last night?'

'Thank you, I did.'

A formal reply. 'If there is anything you need or want to be more comfortable, you just need to say.'

'No, the Rose Room is beautiful and I am very happy there.'

Happy to stay there? Happy to be on her own? Happy to never share his bed?

Uneasiness snaked through him.

'Mrs King has asked if she could show you around Elmsworth Manor today. She is the housekeeper here, whom you met yesterday, and she thought you might wish to take an interest in things?'

'Of course.'

This was said in such a way that implied the very opposite.

She hardly ate anything, either, he saw, merely pouring herself a cup of tea and placing a small bun on her plate.

Was she one of those women who seldom ate?

'There is a garden attached to the kitchen that is interesting.'

'I have no expertise in plants, I am sorry.'

'Then perhaps you might enjoy the piano in the blue salon. Those who use it and are musical always comment on its tone.'

This time she did not give a reply and he kicked himself. When could a young Esther have had the means or the money to learn a musical instrument, tagging along behind her mother as she had in places that were seedy, transient and poor?

The day drew in on him, the storm clouds behind the hills rising, and the feeling that he had made an enormous error lingered over everything.

Would his wife turn out to be a melancholy woman like his mother? That thought had him tucking into the bacon and eggs in front of him. He would eat a big breakfast and stay away from the house for the rest of the day. He had business with the factor of the Elmsworth estate, who had asked for a meeting to go over some of the accounts. If he arranged to see the man at the tavern in the local village, then he could have an excuse ready as to why he had come home late.

He wanted Esther to be the woman who had been on the balcony at the Creighton ball or the one he had met at the Beaumonts' house party, full of chatter and smiles. But she was not that person any more, she was shattered and saddened by a love affair that had ended in public betrayal. He'd have wrung Coulton's neck if he'd been anywhere near him at that second and wrung it gladly.

But he was not. It was only him and Esther marooned at Elmsworth Manor, a place that seemed to bring out the worst in him with all of its memories and its sadness.

He should not have proposed. He should not have raced from Hampshire to London with Mr Curtis in tow and hardly a thought as to how it might actually turn out.

Well, here was the truth of it, two people caught at a breakfast table with nothing to say to each other. A monumental mistake.

Oliver Moreland seemed anxious to be rid of her and she was disappointed that he did not wish to show her the estate himself. He would have had stories and memories she would have loved to hear and through words she might have gained some glimpse into the little boy that now made up the man.

He was busy, she could understand that, lands of this size having demands she could not even fathom. But he asked her nothing about how she felt here or what she might want of this marriage and because of it she had slipped into silence.

They had run out of conversation so very quickly, only ten minutes into a breakfast at the beginning of their first day together. With the Barrington-Halls conversation was the currency of the family's day, never-ending, interesting and thought-provoking. Here so many subjects were suddenly taboo. Childhood. Family. The future. The past.

She even got the strange impression that he did not approve of the breakfast she had chosen, one she had eaten for all the days of her life in Kent with her aunt and uncle.

He on the other hand had stacked his plate high and was making much of tucking into it, his mouth so constantly full there was no chance at all of conversing.

Is this what he wanted?

A silent marriage and one where, after rescuing her from certain ruination, he would now leave her to her own devices?

She swallowed and tried to salvage something of the morning.

'Mrs King said last night that you have dogs here? I heard one barking as I went up the staircase after we arrived yesterday.'

He stopped chewing. 'Indeed. They are my brother's animals.'

'Do they have names?'

'I am not sure. Phillip did tell me, but I can't remember them. Are you fond of dogs?'

'I don't know. My aunt is allergic to anything with fur on and has not encouraged pets.'

'But you hold more affinity to dogs than to horses?'

This time she did laugh, remembering the conversation they had had once about her fear of horses.

'As I have said I was never truly near one.'

He put his knife and fork down and wiped his mouth with the stiff napkin sitting by his plate.

'If you are finished your breakfast, we could go and find out.'

He watched how she scrambled up, her face happier than he had seen it so far, her hair simply plaited so that it fell in a thick blonde rope down her back.

What would it look like unbound and running through his fingers in the candlelight?

Shock had him frowning. She was already wary of him and the last thing he wanted to do was to frighten her further.

Esther quickly picked up on his caution.

'If it is too much trouble…'

But he shook his head. 'I think we will find a dog or two in the kitchen or thereabouts, for according to Mrs King they are always hungry.'

As they entered the kitchen he was called away by his butler with a recently arrived message from his factor and when he returned to the kitchen a few moments later Esther was kneeling down to a black-and-white English Pointer, trying to coax the animal to come to her.

'His name is Percival and the cook has said to be wary of him. I don't know if he likes people much.'

Oliver looked over, the dog's brown eyes watching him. Alarm rose in him for he did not look particularly friendly and he didn't want the animal too

close to Esther. He whistled him over and unexpectedly he came and sat by his left boot.

The dog was thin, his nose long, his ears pricked
in a way that denoted uncertainty.

'He came in from the farm as a puppy,' the cook
continued as she watched the exchange, 'but Her
Ladyship never really took to him as he was too bois-
terous and Lord Elmsworth was always too busy to
take the time to train him.'

Oliver's hand strayed to the head of the dog at
his feet and the animal instantly put its nose into his
palm and licked it.

'Good boy,' he said and Esther began to laugh, a
sound that was true and warm and welcome, no pretence at all within it.

'Perhaps he could be a companion.'

'For us?' He said this with hesitation.

'We could find books and read by the fire at night or
play cards or simply talk. It might make him friendlier.'

This was the most hopeful thing she had said to
him since their wedding and he did not want to dis-
suade conversation.

'If that is what you would like.'

It was the wrong thing to say. He realised that as
soon as he had said it because the light of joy went
from her eyes.

He did not want to sit with her at night and talk.
He didn't want the dog, either. Already he looked as
though he wished to leave, the clothes he wore this
morning country ones, clothes that one strode across

the land in and saw to the many tasks a working farm such as this one might require.

He probably felt trapped here with her, this bland form of domesticity keeping him from the racier entertainments more to his liking.

She wished she might simply ask him what he wanted from this marriage and from her, but the answer might be one which would allow her no peace and at the moment she was still clinging on to other possibilities. He did not look like the man she had known at the London balls or the man whom she had walked with by the river. Here he appeared more like the black-and-white dog at his side, untrusting, hackles up and solitary.

'I should leave you to your work, then, Mr Moreland. I know you must be busy.'

He nodded and left, the dog leaving with him.

The cook looked across at her and smiled.

'Don't worry too much about Percival. He lets nobody close to pat him and so we generally just leave him be. He eats his meal and goes outside as soon as he is able and the gardener has made him a bed in the cottage shed to sleep in at night. He generally returns each morning for breakfast, though sometimes we do not see him for days and days.'

'Where do you think he goes?' she asked, astounded that a pet would not stay close to home, especially in winter.

'A-hunting perhaps, though one of the butlers has seen him a good few miles from here in the local village. Wherever he goes it keeps him thin.'

Esther wished Percival might have stayed with her as a companion. Would her husband be back for lunch, she then wondered, or did he only venture back to the house like the black-and-white dog, when he wanted to? Her future looked as uncertain here as it had in London and she could not work out exactly what to do.

Pulling the ring Oliver Moreland had given her from its place on a chain around her neck, she looked at the ruby, the red within the stone clear and pure. The ring was too big to wear and she did not want to lose it, but he had not offered to get it resized so she had threaded it on to her gold chain this morning for safety. A ring as forgotten as a bride.

She was a wife in name only, his offer to protect her generous in form, but not in execution. She could not write to Charlotte or Sarah, either, for that would feel like a betrayal to Oliver Moreland and besides she wanted no one at all to know of her difficulties.

What could they do except feel sorry for her? Sarah would be in the middle of her own wedding preparations, Charlotte helping as much as she could, her aunt full of plans and giddy organisation.

This was her life now, here at Elmsworth Manor, for better or for worse. She would just have to make the best of it.

Oliver returned to the house after a long day of meetings, the sun well down and a chill in the air. The camaraderie in the village echoed behind him with every step he took, the silence of Elmsworth worrying as he came within it.

'The mistress has decided to eat dinner in her room this evening, sir.' His butler informed him of this as he took his coat and hat, shaking the rain from them both. When the clock behind them struck ten he could well understand why Esther had not waited.

He'd drunk more than he'd meant to, the welcome he'd received from the villagers touching and heart-felt, and when each patron there had bought him another round he'd had little choice but to raise his glass to the many toasts.

Perhaps it was a windfall that his wife had retired, for catching his reflection in the mirror above the mantel he had to admit he looked the worse for wear.

In truth, he did not know quite what to do and staying away from Elmsworth Manor for so many hours was directly responsible for such uncertainty. Should he confront Esther to ask her thoughts on their relationship or should he give her time to get used to the idea that she was here, in Hampshire, married to him until 'death us do part'?

A long time to be unhappy, he thought, his mind going to his father's predicament. After reading the letters given to him by Phillip, Oliver had developed a sympathy for the blustering father that he had never known well or liked much in life. Perhaps such swagger was how he had coped from one day to the next, with a wife whose sickness had crossed over boundaries that it never should have.

God, would he now be put into exactly the same position, trying to mop up the dejection of Esther

Barrington-Hall? He shook his head. She was Esther Moreland now.

'Shall I send supper up to your room, sir?'

Mrs King was beside him, her smile warm.

'No. I will be down in half an hour after I have cleaned up.'

The dog followed him, tail up and head down, its paws on the wooden floors beating out Oliver's pathway as he climbed the stairwell. Percival had stayed by his side all day and he had not the heart now to shoo him off.

When he reached the first landing he saw the door to the Rose Room open and Esther stood there, her face tight with anxiety.

'I thought, perhaps, that you might not be back?'

'I am sorry. I had things to do in the village and time ran away on me.'

Her nostrils flared and he knew she had caught the smell of the alcohol he had consumed even before he saw it in her eyes.

'I am not…drunk.' The ludicrousness of such a statement was not lost on him even as she frowned.

'I have had a tray brought up to my room. There is plenty on it if you would like to join me…?'

'I would.' He blurted that out even as he qualified it. 'But I need to tidy up first if you would give me fifteen minutes.'

Her tight smile was not reassuring. 'I can wait.'

Esther had spent all the afternoon trying to decide how she should handle this awkwardness between them. They were married, that was a fact, and he had been the one to unexpectedly propose. Surely if he regretted such an action now civility would not be too much to ask of him at the very least.

She could not spend her life in this limbo of uncertainty, that much she did know, and she would not simply give up. Her mother had done that time after time when things got hard and by doing so it had all become much worse.

He had been drinking. She could smell it on him even from the distance between them. But he was not drunk. He had said that, too, and in his tone was a sort of worry that was endearing.

Not like her father, then, or the men her mother had gravitated towards, with their lack of sobriety and giving no care for anyone else's feelings apart from their own.

Oliver Moreland had also looked exhausted. She wondered just what he had been doing all day. The dog had been with him, pattering after him like a shadow, its thin frame centred on the man it followed. Was there not some saying that animals could tell a good person from a bad one? She hoped that was true given the hound's loyalty.

In her room she looked at herself in the mirror, giving in to a worry that she needed to appear at her very best. She had not slept well last night, so there was the shadow of that beneath her eyes, but she had dressed carefully and the dark blue in her woollen gown suited her.

She had toyed with the idea of loosening the knot

of her hair at her nape, but then dismissed such vanity because perhaps it could be construed as wanton. She did, however, need to use what God had given her to her best advantage and so applied a slight bit of Charlotte's cream to her lips, but the rosy hue looked wrong under candlelight and so she wiped it off.

Ten minutes now and counting.

The top cover on her bed was askew and she crossed to straighten it. The curtains she had closed as the night fell, the pink in them giving the room a warmth. There was a small fire in the grate and it was giving out a pleasing heat.

The Rose Room. Named for the colour of the curtains and for the wild rose, she supposed, that climbed right around the window frame. She wondered what colour the blooms would be when spring came and then frowned. She might not still be here by spring if she and her new husband did not begin to iron out their differences and start to talk.

Five minutes later he was there, his hair wet and combed back, the dark in it suiting the blue in his eyes. He had changed into more formal clothes, too. He wore a white shirt with a dark waistcoat over the top of it, but with no necktie. His trousers were beige and fitted and his boots were shiny.

She could never quite look at him fully without thinking how very beautiful he was.

His glance went to the clock. Perhaps he did not wish to linger, perhaps he did not want to be here at all? She did not know what to say now that he was right there before her, but he solved the dilemma by speaking.

'I realise we barely know each other, Esther, and I also understand that this marriage of ours has been... hurried, but perhaps if we made an effort to talk things over it might be easier.'

'Things?'

'Worries. Problems. Differences.'

The wind went out of her hope and she stayed silent.

'I know that you were saddened when Lord Coulton did not come up to scratch, but perhaps in the full sense of time you might come to realise that it was for the best. I may be old-fashioned, but I do think that marriage is for ever, no matter what happens, an eternal promise.'

'I do, too.'

'Good.' He looked at her as if she had given him an answer that allowed him to say what he did next. 'Because my mother and father had the sort of marriage which ruined our family life. They never talked about their differences, they just lived them, over and over and for years and years.'

'A grim situation for you and your brother?'

He nodded and stepped forward.

'When I proposed to you it was not entirely out of the blue. I did so because I thought there was something between us, something that drew us to each other that was more than just the unusual meeting in our past. So I ask you now, Esther, if in all honesty you feel even a little bit of the same.'

'I do.'

Breathing out, he went on. 'Then perhaps we could build on that? I could take you around the Elmsworth estate tomorrow to have a look at the land here and to see where I grew up. There are stories and memories which might explain all the things that I am, as well as all the things that I am not.'

He did not touch her. He did not reach out or demand anything. All he wanted was honesty and a chance.

Esther understood that things had changed, that in just the last few moments they had moved on to another place, Oliver Moreland's truths allowing it.

'There was something between us.'

Could it be enough? Could it be a bridge to the sort of life she did want to lead, happily married and content?

'I would enjoy that.'

He nodded and she could see he was thinking of how to go on from here. The dog had curled up on the mat in front of a burning fire and was asleep and when he saw where she looked he smiled.

'Home is where you make it, no matter where you have come from.' His words were said with humour, but they were true, even here in Hampshire at Elmsworth Manor, the rain outside becoming heavier and the branches of the rose bush scratching at her window. When he saw that she was listening to the sound, he explained.

'My mother planted the rose bush when she first came here and it grew and grew.'

'I wondered what colour the flowers were?'

'White. I used to pick her bunches of them and bring them in because it was one of the few things that made her happy.'

His words caught at her and she swallowed. Small acts of hope had been a big part of her childhood, too. Finding objects on the streets—stones, tattered ribbons, wildflowers and suchlike—and bringing them back to Alexandra, placing them at her bedside so that when she woke in the late afternoon she might find them and smile.

An unreliable mother tarnished childhood in a way no one could understand unless you had lived through it. Oliver Moreland apparently had.

'Aunt Mary said that I had to let go of what I could not change when I returned to them after being in London with my mother for all those years.'

'Wise advice.'

'But hard to follow.' She did not wish to skirt across her pain suddenly because for all of her life she had. She had never been truly honest with anyone before and suddenly it was important that she was, with him.

'Alexandra was addicted to obsessions that hurt her. She was not a mother whom one could rely on and so I didn't, and because of her there are things that I am frightened by.'

'Things like blood?'

He looked at her, a line of worry across his brow, and she felt the shock run right through her, keeping her mute.

'At the Beaumonts' house party after Alberton hit me, you were falling...'

'And Benjamin caught me.' She nodded and swallowed. 'I have attacks of panic when I see blood because my mother...shot...herself...' She could not finish, the words simply leaving her, no sound coming.

'Oh, God.'

She felt his hand across her own and held on, because he was an anchor from the past and the only man in the world who could keep her from falling back into the chaos. She clung to him even after the room righted and her breath evened.

The dog had joined them now, sitting nearby and watching, his brown eyes full of concentration and no longer wary. A small family group acting as a buffer against disarray and a shelter of safety.

She met his eyes then, because this had been all so unexpected, her truths difficult ones that she had never shared with anyone before.

But she had always known it would happen with him even from that first second of seeing him again, tall, dark, distant and wild.

There was something there between us and this was it.

She could not quite fathom just what might happen next. The light played on the planes of his face, his eyes darker, all the blue lost. He had a small scar next to his mouth on his right cheek. She had not noticed that before. He had cut himself in his hurry to shave before he came to her room, the dark crust of blood apparent in a nick at his throat.

Every woman in London would have been his bride in a heartbeat, every young girl in society imagining what it would be like to have a husband like Oliver Moreland and indeed a few of the older ones as well.

But he had chosen her, asked her to be his wife and he had qualified it with the simple reasoning that he thought there was something between them. She could not let that go without a fight.

She had no experience of the sensual, no idea how to instigate it, either, but his hand was in hers and real, his fingers curled around her own, holding her close.

The room all around drew in, the shadows of the candle, the smell of the fire, the soap he had used before coming to her room that was scented with lavender. Perhaps picked from the kitchen gardens here, in the summer, as the bushes bloomed along the borders.

When he brought her hand up his mouth grazed the back of it. She felt his lips there, felt what he asked, felt the honesty, too, not one packaged in betrayal as Lord Coulton's had been, but framed with hope.

The hope for more moments like these.

'Sometimes one must take a risk to live, Esther, for if you dare nothing, then nothing is all you will have.' He spoke softly.

'My mother was risky—' she said, but he did not let her finish.

'Your mother made poor choices, but you can make good ones.'

He was right. Good choices, even if they were risky, were less liable to veer off into the unsafe.

He kissed her hand again, not pushing, not expecting, but in the manner of a husband who was prepared to wait.

Esther did not quite know how to go on from here, how to make him understand that she did want more, all the worries of being frigid and frightened disappearing under his touch.

Her aunt's words were also on her mind. Unlike Alexandra and Esther's father, this union had started from an equal footing as man and wife, both damaged by their pasts, both wary of commitment, but honesty had also crept in and with it came the promise of more.

The dog barked and they laughed, Oliver Moreland letting go of her fingers and calling Percival to his side.

'I think he is hungry and I am, too,' he said, looking at the food on the table behind them, one of cheese and meats and fresh crusty breads.

This was easy, she thought, as she brought the tray over and set it in front of them.

He did not pounce on her like Lord Coulton or make her feel uncomfortable as Lord Alberton had been wont to do. No, he held himself back even while stating what he wanted.

Esther poured the wine from the jug into two glasses and when he lifted his, she did, too.

'Here's to us, then.' The smile in his words were exactly what she needed.

Picking up a piece of meat, he handed it to Percival and the dog gulped it down in a second.

'He stayed with me all day. I was in the village pub

having a meeting with the Elmsworth factor after looking over the lands. We went back to have a drink with the locals because unless you keep in touch with the men who work your property you can miss things.'

'Such as?'

'The births. The deaths. The problems that can be fixed with a single conversation. But they kept buying me another round and I could not refuse.'

'It sounds as if you like it here?'

'Maybe I do, but Phillip will come back one day and this is his life.'

'Does your brother enjoy it?'

'I'm not sure. He's let the place go a bit, to be honest, and there are decisions he has made that I would not have, but it's been a long time since we have sat together and really talked. His wife is sick, though I doubt he wants anyone to know that, and she wishes to be with her parents in Virginia. I got the impression that it will be terminal.'

'Well, your brother is by her side to help her and he won't regret that.'

'Do you miss the Barrington-Hall family, Esther?'

'Of course. Family is the most important thing that you ever have in life.'

'You believe this to be true even after all you went through?'

'I do.'

'My own sort of fell to pieces and Phillip and I could never reassemble the scattered bits. Lately I have wondered if I should have tried harder.'

He frowned and she saw he was pondering over

what to say next. 'My brother left me a folder full of my father's thoughts written down over several years. He was a blustery, stern man who was violent at times and distant at others, but I never realised his problems. I think my mother may have been slightly mad.'

'Mine was more than slightly mad. By the end of her life I wondered if Alexandra had ever been sane at all. She left her family home at eighteen to marry my father and never contacted my grandparents again. Her betrayals broke her parents' hearts and they died shortly afterwards. Then when my father died she cut all ties with the Barrington-Halls as well and disappeared to London with me.'

'A poor decision.' He said the words kindly, though.

'Mama did not take well to anyone advising her what to do, and Aunt Mary does have a tendency to give her opinion, though I am sure she meant it for the best. She wanted Alexandra to leave me with them until she had worked out her life. When she did not the Barrington-Halls made it be known that my mother had gone north, though they knew she had done no such thing.'

'Our secret dilemmas.'

'Not so secret, now.'

'But safe, none the less.'

When he smiled at her summation she felt as if the world was at her feet to make of herself just who she liked. Usually when she spoke of her mother the anxiety built, but tonight it did not and she understood it was because he had shared his own story.

Outside the storm continued to batter the house,

lightning and thunder in the distance. But in here it was calm and warm, the firelight dancing, the dog, Percival, asleep now across her new husband's boots and snoring lightly.

Protection had a snugness to it and a security that was rare. Esther had not thought to feel this again outside the Barrington-Hall family, but she did and every bit as powerfully. It was a gift that astonished her because in the knowing was the kernel of a future she had not expected.

'I used to imagine a life like this when I was little, but then I stopped believing because everything became so topsy-turvy.'

'Were you hurt at any time, Esther, when you were with your mother?'

He was still as he waited for her reply.

'No. I hid a lot.'

'Hell.' He did not say this kindly.

'Once a man tried to kiss me, but he was drunk and it was easy to escape.'

'If I had children, I would protect them with my life and would never allow anyone near who could bring them harm.'

She saw the fury in him like a beacon and her tears welled.

'You helped me when I needed you, for I don't know what would have happened if you had not come and it was better after that for a time…'

He saw the memories flit across her face and the darkness in her eyes. Esther had been a thin, frightened twelve-year-old when he had come across her seven years after her mother had left the protection of her family and there would be another year or two before she would be returned.

He wanted to move forward and take her in his arms, but he could see she was fighting back tears and would not have appreciated more emotion.

So instead he chose the one topic that she herself had mentioned in an effort to take her mind away from sadder things.

'Do you play chess?'

She looked up and he saw relief in her eyes. 'I do. My uncle taught me and the Barrington-Halls are all highly competitive.'

'I shall have to work for victory, then. Give me a moment to get the board from my bedchamber and I will be back.'

Three hours later Oliver lay in his bed, staring at the ceiling, unable to sleep.

He could not get the image of a young Esther from his mind and when she had answered his question about if she had been hurt by anyone he had wanted to fall to his knees and thank the Lord above that she had been spared the sort of fate many other little girls might not have been. Images of the children at the St Mary's Home came to mind and he rolled up to sit on his bed.

Outside it was still raining, but the evening had been one he would never forget.

When he had returned with the chessboard they

had sat playing the game and it had taken all his concentration to beat her. He'd been the chess champion at school and had played it often since, so her prowess was welcomed.

She had laughed at his antics in a way that had made him laugh, too, and he'd thought he did not wish to be anywhere else in the world except there in her room, watching her. Always with every other woman he had spent some time with he had known it would be a finite thing, a day, a week, a month, but never any more.

He shook his head. He had played the field for years, a tumbling rolling stone, never wanting to settle, always keeping his distance, careful in what he said and showed.

But with Esther he was content and the constraints of the past seemed to wash away.

His ring was threaded now on a gold chain around her neck, he saw, and it suited her. Her fingers had often reached up and cradled the ruby as she played and every time she did that it made him smile. An unconscious gesture that denoted attachment and even the dog had crept over to her and laid its head in her lap.

She had been delighted, gesturing for him to notice Percival's attention and smiling broadly.

This is what home and belonging felt like, he thought then in shock. Just this. In the morning he would look for a more suitable wedding ring and one at least that had the possibility of fitting.

Chapter Twelve

She woke to the new day and saw that the sun shone and the sky was largely blue. A pleasing thing because Oliver Moreland was going to show her the lands of the estate today, on horseback.

Did that mean she would be in front of him or behind him in the saddle? Whatever position, she knew it would be close.

He had kissed her hand again at the end of the night, thanking her for the game of chess and leaving quickly, and though she'd wished he might linger his eyes were hooded and she could not tell anything at all from the expression on his face.

He was good at hiding things, she thought, and keeping a distance, though he had seemed content to spend the evening with her. She had nearly beaten him at chess, too, but had faltered on the final moves as him glance had met hers in a way that could only be described as sensual. He had captured her queen then, without too much trouble at all.

Sitting up, she glanced around her room and saw Percival the dog on the mat almost under her feet.

'You slept with me last night?'

Her voice woke him and he looked up, his golden eyes soft and his tail thumping on the ground behind him. Delight filled her and, unable to sit still for a moment longer, she rang her bell and waited for the maid to come to help her dress.

She'd wear her green riding habit, for the cut and colour made it one of her favourites, and she would get the maid to dress her hair in an informal style, braiding the top layer and letting the rest fall loose. The thick wool in her jacket would keep the warmth in and the wind out and her boots would allow for any walking they might do on their journey.

Everything felt exciting and hopeful, having her husband's uninterrupted company for a whole day, the kisses he had placed on her hand last night putting a new slant on the outing. Perhaps away from others he might kiss her properly, reach out and bring her into his warmth. She felt the hope of it inside her, an unfamiliar ache building, and she crossed her arms to keep the feeling in.

Two hours later they were at the stables and her husband had led his enormous black stallion out.

'He looks fierce.' Up close the animal was scarier than she had remembered, muscles everywhere rippling and his breath white in the cold of the day.

'He won't hurt you, Esther. He is well trained.'

'By you?'

He smiled and held out his hand.

'I will help you mount and then I will come up behind you.'

She placed her fingers in his, feeling the warmth, and he led her to the horse's side.

'Put your foot here,' he said and waited till she did before lifting her up with ease, her other leg coming across the body of the animal and suddenly she was there clinging with all she was worth to the edges of the saddle. Without any effort at all he swung up behind her, the strength of his arms now around her, his body at her back.

A startlingly intimate position that had his thighs coming beside hers.

'We will go slow at first so you can get used to it.'

'It's very high up.'

'Have you never once been on a horse?'

'I haven't. My uncle wanted me to learn when I returned to Kent, but I never had the inclination or the courage.'

'What did you like doing?'

She smiled because she knew he was trying to keep her mind on things other than her fear as he walked his horse forward.

'Well, I learnt the game of chess and read a lot. For a few years anyway the peace of Redworth Manor was wonderful and after that I pottered about with the family and then joined my girl cousins in their schoolroom lessons.'

'Were you well when you came back, Esther? You looked very thin when I first saw you?'

She shook her head and felt the dread of it mar the day. 'I got anxious for a long time and I still do sometimes, but much more rarely than before.'

She was glad she was not looking at him as she said this, but today she had promised that she would be truthful if he asked her things and so she was going to be.

'How did your uncle discover you in London after all those years?'

'He had been looking for a while. After my mother died I was sent to an orphanage and he found me there. I had my mother's Bible with me, you see, and on seeing the family coat of arms inside the front cover the matron began to make enquiries.'

His arms tightened about her as the horse's speed quickened and the wind came into her hair, a wild freedom that took her breath away. He was a skilful rider. She could feel his thighs guiding the stallion and the small shifts of his weight to indicate direction.

No wonder Charlotte loved horses, Esther suddenly thought, if this was the feeling one got when on their backs, the miles swallowed easily and the landscape changing. It was not a frightening thing at all, but an exhilarating freedom that made her laugh out loud.

'You like it?' His words were taken by the wind even as he said them.

'I do.'

Finally, they slowed and stopped just beneath the rise of one of the many hills, in the shelter of a grassy bank cut into a slope leading down to a field. Before her was the whole vista of the place—the house, the lake, the farm and the trees lining the seams of the valley. A verdant green undulating land dotted with cows and sheep and crops carefully planted.

Like a small kingdom.

He helped her down after he had dismounted, hands around her waist as he lowered her to the ground. She was tall for a girl, but he was much taller and she liked that he was. She liked the feel of him, too, there against her.

'This is the best view of the place. I used to come here when I was young and stay for hours, but I have not been back in a long while.'

'Because you were busy in town?'

'And because when I left here the last time I meant never to return. Your family had their fractures, Esther, but so did mine. I think I told you my father was a difficult man, but I did not actually say why.'

He didn't look at her as he said this and she felt a quick jolt of worry.

Oliver wanted to tell her who he was, what he was. He wanted to let her know about all the secrets held in the leather-bound book that Phillip had given him before he had left for America. He wanted to let Esther understand his past out here in the open under the sky of the Elmsworth lands and with no chance of any interruption.

For the first time in all his life distance seemed like a mistake and unless he told Esther the truth he believed he might never recover.

She had been honest about her attacks of anxiety

and about her childhood and he needed to be, too, if they were to live out of the shadows in a marriage that stood a chance.

'My mother tried to kill Phillip and me on a number of occasions. The last time she nearly succeeded and had it not been for my father happening down to the lake just as the boat we were on tipped over, we would have drowned. It was windy, you see, and Mama had picked a day when we would have had no chance of reaching the shore.'

He saw Esther watching him, pain in her eyes, and when she reached out to take his hand in her own he held on because there was more to say and a lot of it.

'Phillip let go first and tried to swim to our mother, but the waves were high and he kept being pulled under. My father got to him and brought him to the boat, laying him on the upturned hull and beating the water from his chest. My brother was half-conscious and Papa could only rescue one of them without sacrificing the other, the choice showing on his face in a terrible way. I watched my mother floating on her back, her hair trailing out behind her. She was wearing a nightgown and it billowed out as if her thinness was suddenly cured but then she began to sink and my father shouted at her again and again until she was gone and the evening dark fell on all of us taking away the light.'

'How did you get back to the shore?'

'My father held us both and began kicking and bit by bit we drifted in, by which time help had come down from Elmsworth Manor in the form of servants holding fired torches, and the rescue began.'

'It's why you don't like deep lakes? You told me that once.'

He smiled. 'I wondered if you might remember.'

'She didn't want to live? Your mother?'

'No, but she didn't want to die alone, either. I used to imagine a mother who cared for us, nurtured us, wanted us, until Phillip gave me a book full of my father's letters recently. Then I remembered the lake and what she had looked like as she overturned the boat and I knew it was the truth. Melancholy is a drug far worse than anything your mother ever took, I think, Esther, and at least yours tried to keep you safe.'

'A generous thought, even if a little misguided, but I thank you for it.'

He laughed because in the middle of tragedy, humour helped.

'But I am coming to realise that there is a time to leave the past behind us and live, Mr Moreland, and perhaps that time is now.'

'Oliver.'

'I like that name.' Her voice was soft and the dimples in her cheeks were easy to see.

'Love me, Esther. Love me until I forget.'

The words came without hesitation, almost without thought, pulled from inside like living things, and she stilled, the wind in her hair, her eyes a colour that always surprised him.

The breath of his words was against her face, so close she could breathe them in and she did.

'I will.'

One finger came to her cheek, tracing the shape down to her dimple and feeling the indent.

'You are so very beautiful.'

Many men had said that to her in the salons of her first Season and the words had never seemed real. But these ones were. She felt her whole body still in the seconds of waiting.

'I want our marriage to last, Esther.'

'For ever,' she whispered back, and then everything changed, instantly, the shock of the sensual, which had always been so frightening, now threaded in heat instead, an intensity so torrid she would have fallen had he not caught her to him.

His mouth came down across her own, not the small kiss that Lord Coulton had offered, full of a cold nothingness, but a passionate, honest kiss, one of his hand behind her head and the other against her cheek holding her there. A man's kiss, a lover's kiss, need and lust written across it, but underpinned with something gentler.

His desire was not tempered by manners, but was given in hunger, and when he changed the angle by moving his head she simply went to pieces under his expertise, the fluid honesty of his embrace making her press into him and open her mouth wider.

She wanted him as much as he wanted her, no barriers, no limits, only them on the hillside overlooking the lands of Elmsworth in the breeze of the afternoon and under the quiet warmth of a late winter sun.

She heard herself groan as his tongue came in to

explore, the tempo quickening, his grip on her harder
and her centre splintering out into flame.

She needed him in the manner that women had
understood across the centuries. He was hers and she
was his and though she could not quite understand
what was meant to happen, her body was threaded
with a wordless yearning.

He stilled her then by bringing her in against him,
one hand splayed across her back. She could hear the
beating drum of his heart, fast and hard, a tempo the
same as her own.

'God.' One word breathed into her ear and then
more. 'It can't be here, Esther. It would not be right.'

But the heat between them was not to be tempered
by right or wrong, the thundering truth of this moment or nothing at all in both of their ears, the pro-
saic and predictable destroyed entirely by the fierce
quicksilver of need.

He held her up against the rising cut of land and
sheltered her against the wind, his breath rough now
and broken, no longer the urbane, controlled man
that she knew, no longer the city aristocrat with all
of the answers. Not a game, either, nor some ruled
discourse that encompassed distance, and no gleam
in his eye that told her he knew exactly what he was
doing.

He looked as lost as she was, on new ground that
had shocked him as much as it had her, his expression vulnerable, the pulse in his throat fast.

'I want you, Esther.'

No lies in this, no platitudes.

'I want you, too.' She whispered the words through delight.

He thrust one leg forward so that it rested against the cliff and then he brought her across him, lifting her skirts as he did so, only the thin lawn of her petticoat shielding her from the hard warmth she felt there.

A man's body, nothing hidden. When he rocked against her she understood what it was he was asking, a question that did not require words, and his mouth came across her throat, tasting her, marking her. She could feel his tongue gentling the pain and her legs opened further. Then he moved again, one hand coming under her skirt, along her thigh and then in between her legs, searching for the place that called him, the throb in a rhythm of want, a noise bursting from her lips that she had never heard herself make before, a groan full of pure need.

His fingers answered, pushing their way into her very centre, into the heat of her and the wetness. She could feel her muscles tightening around him, holding him there, her thighs clamping together to keep him still as she simply went to pieces, letting go of the world and spiralling up and up to a place that was devoid of everything, save bliss and wonder and marvel.

She had neither breath nor sight, her eyes shut, the darkness pulsating and primal in a rebirth and a cleansing.

This was the truth inside her that had clambered to escape, a truth that allowed hope and courage and possibility, and was no longer bound by other people and their problems, no echoes even of the past.

She began to cry as his hand left her and he pulled
her into his arms. She wanted him back again, back
to where she could keep him all for herself, the hidden folds of her body around his warmth.

'Shh...' he said and stroked her hair, fallen from
the pins now, her hat askew, the length of her wild
wind-blown tresses binding them.

Hell. His wife was more enticing than any woman
he had ever bedded. She was alive with sensuality and
a lust that floored him, nothing held back or muted,
no small response that put up barriers to the honest
hot-blooded truth that took his breath away.

She was crying because she wanted him back, she
told him so in as many words as he tried to calm her.
She clutched him to her, and he could feel her curves
and her desire still, her breath against his throat fast
and shallow and desperate.

Her hair in all shades of honey and wheat and
whiteness swirled around them, the length astonishing, and when her tongue licked his throat and her
mouth came against his neck to suck in the manner
he had shown her a few minutes before, he took her
down with him on to the grass.

She watched him with those eyes of hers, languid,
dangerous and green like a witch's glance, knowing
full well what she was asking, the spell of lust upon
them both and growing.

He would teach her all that she sought. He would
love her with every part of his body, properly and
without limit.

He watched her face as he undid the buttons on her riding jacket, the white shirt beneath thin and gauzy. Undoing the smaller row of buttons, he took in a breath as her breasts rode high and naked, her nipples hardening of their own volition.

His to take. She did not move as his hand cupped one breast, his fingers flicking at the bud in a rhythm that spoke of other things. Then her flesh was in his mouth, tasting sweet as she stretched like a cat wanting to be stroked, her mouth open, every part of her body waiting for what might come next.

He felt like Adam in the Garden of Eden, instructing Eve in the very first days of the world. He felt as if Esther had been created only for him, his wife, his love, his woman from now on until eternity.

'I would never want to hurt you, but what we will do might be painful…for a moment…before it becomes beautiful.'

'Like you?'

Smiling he lifted her skirt, the fabric pooling around his hands. Her lacy garters holding the stockings lay beneath, like a symbol of the innocence he knew her to have.

She moved her legs apart, bending her knees so that he could see what was there, drawers of fine lawn and nothing else.

The wind was on her thighs and between her legs, open to the sky and to the hands of her husband. She watched as he took off his coat, boots and breeches, the necktie following in a single band of cotton wafting in the breeze.

In just a long white shirt he leant down and opened her legs, taking her in his mouth, the shock of it making her try to sit even as he began to kiss her there, even as his other hand kept her still.

'No, my love, it is my turn now,' he said as he raised his head just for a second and she did as he asked, eyes wide in wonder as she moved with him, her fingers entwined in his hair, her thighs a startling white against the day, her stockings now strewn on the grass, along with her boots, garters and drawers.

Undone, undressed and unbelievably taken, by love and lust and excitement. And just as she wondered if she could take any more he stopped, his arms coming under her hips as he tipped her up, a different angle from before, and brought her legs around his, the hard urgency of him against her, flesh swollen in want.

'I will always protect you,' he said solemnly as he waited at the entrance of the place where his fingers had just been.

'I know,' she gave him back, and his restraint broke, his manhood coming in, slowly, until a sharp stab of pain made him wait before plunging in as far as he could, deep inside and then deeper again.

She moved with him, knowing instinctively what to do, the beauty of this dance gentle and fierce and unstoppable. She understood what was wanted as the tempo built and quickened until there was nothing left that held them apart, only a togetherness that bound them, melded them, kept them as a single entity while the blood surged in waves of release through their bodies, throbbing with belonging.

She was his and he was hers, husband and wife, man and woman. She had never felt so whole.

He held her then, his arms wrapped tight about her, rolling her to one side so that his weight was not upon her, but so she was protected and warm. Re-buttoning her shirt and jacket, he tucked the hood around her hair. In this light it looked blonder than he had ever seen it and her eyes against the wide sky greener.

'You are beautiful both inside and out, Esther.'

Her dimples showed. 'I love you, Oliver. I have loved you from the moment we first met. You have always been my knight in shining armour.'

Her words were full of honesty and he could not believe she would be brave enough to say them like that, just the truth as she knew it.

'I love you, too.'

He had never said those words to anyone. He had barely ever thought them.

Her finger traced the line of his cheek, warm against his cold. 'When love is shared everything is possible.'

'Things like hope and trust and faith? I never had any of those things before. I think I was lost…' He stopped.

'But now we are found here at Elmsworth.'

He remembered his aunt's words. *'Go to Elmsworth to recover. It is the only place you will.'* Perhaps they had been true. Perhaps until you could face what had been taken from you, you could not understand what you had been given.

Esther. His world now. His reason for living.

He took her to his bed that night, his chamber in the eaves of the second storey, an escape high up in the roofline overlooking the lawns and the lake.

'My room always seemed too big and dark when I was young and too far away up here in the roof. I used to fashion a bed over there on the window seat and watch the sky because this room seemed as if it should have more people in it than just me.'

They were tucked up under the feather quilt his mother had made when she was happier, a fire in the grate burning down and the eternal rain at the window.

'And now it has us both.' He could hear the laughter in her voice.

'Did you love Coulton, Esther? Barrett said Sarah told him you cried for him every night after he betrayed you.'

She shook her head. 'My cousin may be clever, Oliver, but she has no idea of human behaviour. I cried because you had not put your name on the list of suitors my uncle had furnished me with and because you were lost to me for ever.' She propped herself up as she went on, her head on one hand so that she could look at him properly. 'He kissed me and I hated it and I thought there must be something wrong with me, but I could not tell anyone because by then we were engaged…'

'I am glad to hear that you were not heartbroken, my love. I thought you did not seem happy when I came to the party your aunt and uncle put on for your engagement. I wondered why no one else could see it.'

'I hated that night. I wished you would simply take my hand and run away with me, from everyone and everything.'

'God, how I wanted to, but I thought I was protecting you by letting you go.'

Her body glowed in the firelight, pale and feminine, her eyes catching the flame as he kissed her.

'I have loved you always, Oliver. I thought right from the first time I saw you that you were the most beautiful man who ever lived. When you came down the steps at the Creighton ball and the conversation stopped, it was as if I knew that one day you would be mine and that we were linked somehow.'

He laughed. 'Even given my reputation as a wild and dissolute second son?'

'Were you, though? It never quite made sense to me after you had saved Mama and me that night.'

'Perhaps once I was, but in the last few years other things have been more important. I fund a children's home in Whitechapel, a place that helps find work and provide education for lost children. A place that gives them back a future.'

'Did protecting vulnerable children have anything at all to do with helping me on the street all those years ago?'

He nodded. 'I think it did. After leaving you in

Camden Town that night I vowed to make my life finer and more purposeful.'

'My cousin Jeremy talked once of seeing you in the middle of the night turning into the streets there. He imagined you were visiting a lover, I think, or dealing in illicit drugs.'

'People see what they want to or what is expected. I have slept with a good number of women in my time, but I always kept something back. With you, my love, that is impossible.'

'I am so glad that you have helped others in need. Many of the suitors who plied for my hand were greedy or self-centred and would not have even imagined doing such work. Will you keep it on?'

'Yes, and you can help me if you want. We will stay here until I get Elmsworth Manor into some sort of financial shape and then I will employ someone to run it and we can go back to London. I have a place in Westminster, but if that address is not somewhere you would be comfortable with I can buy us another.'

'Is it near the park?'

He nodded.

'Then I shall love it. You can teach me to ride and we can have picnics there in the summertime and walk in the evenings.'

'I also want to find a country place. Something old and beautiful and with enough land to farm. Phillip will come back to Elmsworth and he will need some company.'

'Then perhaps we could find something close by.'

He reached out to sweep her hair back and kissed

her on the shoulder. She was not wearing a nightgown
and because of it he trailed lower. And then lower
again.

'I love you,' he said simply.

'Show me all the ways you do, my darling.'

'With pleasure,' he returned.

And then he could no longer think of anything.

Epilogue

Nettleford Park, Hampshire
—Christmas 1819

Oliver smiled. Around him on all the chairs and settles in the main salon sat family and friends, full after an early Christmas supper, the table still heaving with uneaten food, decorations on the mantel in green and gold and a yule log sitting in front of a fire that had almost gone down to ash.

'You have the look of a man who suits country life, Oliver,' Barrett said, Sarah beside him, their small daughter asleep in her arms. 'I expected you to be much more exhausted with your growing brood. I know I certainly am.'

Oliver glanced across the room at Esther, the almost one-year-old Juliette playing at her feet and their three-year-old son, William, at the table, a spoon in his hand finding yet another mouthful of something delicious.

He loved them so much that it hurt.

'My growing brood as you put it is the source of much joy and I finally feel content. Freddie sent word that he is in Exeter, by the way, and will make it up here to Nettleford with his wife by the second week of January.'

Barrett smiled. 'Oh, how times have changed. Remember those young bucks we once were without a care in the world?'

'And remember the sheer loneliness of it, too? I wouldn't change this life for anything.'

Mary Duggan next to her husband on the other side of the room caught his glance, raising her glass to him.

'Here's to us all, Oliver, and to many, many more good times.'

He drank at her toast. As the matriarch of the large and close Barrington-Hall family, Mary had taught him a lot about the machinations of family life, the prickly beginnings between them settling into a close relationship.

Charlotte grabbed William as he ran by her and spun him around and their son's laughter filled the room. Esther's cousin had come to live with them after a disappointment with some suitor and she had looked happier and happier as the year had progressed. This Christmas she had spent a lot of time with Michael Tomlinson, who had arrived injured from London after a riot in Whitechapel. They were both often in each other's company and there was a new lightness in his friend which was good to see. He knew Esther was hoping that marriage was in their future.

Julia was busy helping Juliette place a pile of blocks one on top of another, his daughter squealing with delight as they fell with a clatter. His aunt had been a huge help with the children, and she was here at Nettleford Park more often than not.

Oliver walked over to his wife, and Esther glanced at him in that certain way that said tonight after everyone had retired she would be happy to be with him alone in the big bed they had had brought from Elmsworth Manor.

His arm came around her shoulders and she moved closer, the swell of her stomach more noticeable than ever. Another baby due in March, three little ones in as many years. He could not believe his fortune.

'You look happy,' he said, kissing her on the cheek.

'Because I am.' A slight sadness filled her green eyes. 'He didn't come? Again?'

'Maybe next year,' he returned, thinking of Phillip. It had been almost four years since he had heard from his brother, despite sending letters, and he'd thought that perhaps this Christmas…

'I love you,' she said, seeing his thoughts and glancing at the clock. 'There is still time…'

He shook his head. 'He will come, but not this year. Besides, I have everything I need in you and the children.'

As if on cue his son wandered over and Oliver picked him up and held him close. Juliette had begun to cry, but before Esther could see to her, Julia had her in a warm embrace.

He had everything that made life worth living and

more and when the ruby ring he had given Esther glinted from its chain at her neck he lifted her left hand and kissed the large green emerald on her finger that he had had made especially as a replacement wedding ring.

'To us,' he said, 'and Merry Christmas, my darling.'

'I love you, Oliver.' She gave these words back in a way that made him feel like the knight in shining armour she so very often said that he was.

Happiness was just this, family and friends celebrating the season on a snowy late afternoon in their country house in Hampshire.

His whole life had come full circle, for Elmsworth Manor was only a matter of a few miles from here. Love had brought him home and it kept him here, contented, settled and satisfied.

Leaning over, he took two long fluted glasses of wine from the tray behind him and passed one to Esther.

'To us,' he said and drank.

'For ever,' she returned, and the words made him smile in delight.

* * * * *